The Best of the Flashes

Paul John Hausleben

Cover design, and cover concept by Paul John Hausleben

Photographs of the author are by Ms. Cali Rose

Logos, drawings, and images are by Paul John Hausleben

All stories written by Paul John Hausleben

Any scripture references are from: The Holy Bible, King James Version. Cambridge Edition: 1769. Public Domain

Published by God Bless the Keg Publishing LLC

Henrico, Virginia, U.S.A.

ISBN: 979-8-9894490-5-7

Dedication

"To Old Sparky, the screwdriver, whose career slowly evolved from being a big screwdriver to being a circuit breaker tester. And to 6LQ6 high output vacuum tubes and flyback transformers. Youse guys epitomized teamwork and really knew how to create some flashes, sparks, and shorts."

The Best of the Flashes

Paul John Hausleben

Contents

Previously Unpublished Flashes

Acknowledgements

Thank you to Mr. Harry M. Rogers Junior. Thank you for the flashes and sparks and shorts in my life. In many ways, those elements set me off in dual directions in my life.

"A home must have books. Or it is just not a home."

Paul John Hausleben

November 2025

Author Notes

I built my first ham radio from a kit when I was about ten years of age (with keen assistance from my old man and my Uncle Ed) and in doing so, I fell in love with radio and with electricity and electronics. That radio changed my life and set me off on a lifetime of fun and memories and joy associated with radio. A career, too.

In my career of working as an electrician and an electronics technician, while attempting to capture and control electrons and then subsequently and strategically running away from electrons to prevent them from nipping me in the backside, I learned to respect the power of the flashes of electrons! Sometimes, I learned the hard way. I always admired the finger-licking guys, who had the courage to lick their very calloused fingers and dance them along the edges of bare copper wires and detect electrons. I never had the skill or the courage; however, I did have some calloused fingers in my days.

Controlling the flashes, sparks, and shorts proved to be tricky and strategic.

When I first dabbled in flash fiction and wrote a flash fiction piece, I fell in love with this type of writing. Creating stories and characters within a few words suited my writing career at that time. I needed a break from the arduous task of composing themes, the writing, the production, and the editing of novels. There remained a duality between my work with electrons and my work with words. I respected the power of both.

They both have flashes associated with them. Both

suited my career path.

Much to my surprise, I ended up composing five volumes of flash fiction pieces, mixed with the inspirational and often humorous pieces we called sparks, and some short stories.

Over the sharing of some beers, (that seems to be a pattern of inspiration in my life) a close friend reminded me of how many of the Flashes, Sparks, and Shorts that I wrote. He suggested that a "Best of the Flashes" would do well for the readers at this time. It was his thought that it would help to introduce readers to this unusual and uncommon type of writing.

Additionally, to provide a boost to the potential project, I did have about ten flash fiction pieces hidden in the PJH Writing Vault that remained unpublished.

Paulie had just completed *Snow on the Roof*, which was the final Detective Lyle Odell novel in the Odell series; therefore, an easier and stress-free project seemed like a very good idea! Henceforth, I set forth with a careful study of the many flash fiction pieces in the five collections, along with an assist with the selections by a fellow God Bless the Keg Publishing LLC associate, and we selected what we thought were the best of the lot.

Then, after unlocking the vault, we selected the best of the unpublished pieces.

And because of my experience and knowledge of those tricky electrons, I knew that to have a few flashes, we needed a short.

For that purpose, I picked a short story from a now very old, out-of-print short story collection. A piece that I always felt was an overlooked piece and a piece that had some powerful emotions associated with it.

PJH and the GBTKP LLC team worked on some artwork

and a new GBTKP LLC logo for the covers and some other PJH photos to grace the books. And here we are. *The Best of the Flashes.*

I really enjoy that the subjects, the cast of characters, and the general themes for these flash fiction pieces wander all over the place within the genre spectrum. In these flash fiction pieces, within a few short words, we touch many aspects of human emotions and situations. We have some holiday celebrations; we have some romance, some religion, a little touch of reality situations, some drama, some tugging at the heartstrings, and of course, my trademark off-beat humor. There are no limitations or rules for the genres; Paulie just writes whatever pops into his head at the time.

I think that in the review of the selections of these pieces for this collection that we did manage to capture all aspects of the exceptional joy of the journey that we call life and the emotions and the adventures that we all share together.

That fact gives me great happiness.

Will Paulie write some more flash fiction? Time will tell. In the meantime, we have these collections to enjoy. That is until I decide to wander off into the world of brevity of words and depictions of whatever pops into my mind once more.

I enjoyed composing this collection of stories and writing a few new ones, too. I hope you enjoy reading them as much as I enjoyed the experience of writing them.

Thank you for reading them.

Paul John Hausleben

November 2025

Her Jeans Were Tight Now

From: Flashes, Sparks, and Shorts: Flash One

Her jeans were tight now.

She pulled them on and wiggled a bit, sucked in hard and then worked the button on the waist closed.

'It is more that I just washed them rather than the fact I have gained weight,' she thought.

She remained partly convinced that was true. When in doubt, always accuse the laundry shrinkage as the culprit for the tight waist.

She wiggled a bit more, squatted down in an effort to loosen them, and tugged at the legs to encourage a bit of a stretch in the newly washed jeans. In front of the mirror, she checked out her backside and spun around and in a wave of self-examination; she thought she looked rather sexy. A new blouse easily slipped over her; it was on sale yesterday. A V-neck to reveal just a whisper of modest cleavage. The blouse was light and airy, with a touch of frill along the sleeves, intensely black in color, and she loved it. Black jeans, black blouse, and a pair of black dress boots with an illusion of a high-heel.

She also knew that all he wore was black.

Always.

Supposition mixed with evidence to lead her to the belief that black was his thing. A new haircut, not too short, but the stylist convinced her to go trendy and allow a touch of a wave of hair to cross her face.

"If you do not want to do the sexy stare through the wave of hair, tuck it behind your ear. Make sure that you highlight your eyes and lashes with liner and stare out at him. You're gonna melt this dude," was the stylist's advice.

She went with it and she dyed her hair a shade or two off her natural color, because there was a hint of gray along the edges and here and there. The finishing touches were her grandmother's heirloom hoop earrings, and the matching single gold chain of a necklace that she just had to wear. They were not expensive pieces; they were slightly tarnished pieces of gold, with some waves of mystery involved in them. She was very close to Grammy, and she missed her every day. Through hints, parts, and pieces of conversation, she was sure that a special lover gave the pieces to her grandmother. Maybe before Grandpa was in the picture, or maybe not. Just the manner in which Grammy held them in her hands and stared at them with this love-struck look in her eyes made her sure that she was correct in her assumption. He must have been the love of her life, and these were precious reminders. Grammy left them to her in her will because Grammy knew that her granddaughter knew the true history of the pieces. Now, they were going to bring her luck today with the unapproachable man in black.

Every Sunday he was there for brunch.

Today was Sunday.

He would be there today. At the end of the bar, sitting alone, nursing a beer, chatting occasionally with the bartender, or a server that he seemed to know for a long time, but mostly remaining silent and pensive. Always dressed in black, perfect in his features, stunning in appearance. She had never seen a more handsome man than he was. At a guess, he was at least ten years older than she was . . . he was one of those lucky people that it was impossible to tell how old he was. Their age meant nothing. She couldn't care less. Her heart would go pitter-patter at the sight of him. They had only very scant bits of conversation in the past. She would always say something stupid and irrelevant. He would smile, comment, and say a few polite words with his hard New Jersey accent and then he would fade away. As soon as she tried to break the ice, it would freeze over once more.

From milking information from the bartender who was a gal she trusted and knew (and who, despite best efforts, had no success in her own pursuit of the same man) for a long time, he loved music . . . primarily classic rock-and-roll. He was a fan of ice hockey too. His server friend coughed up that tidbit. Other than those subjects, the inside scoop well ran dry. He never spoke of much else other than general subjects. No one even knew what he did for a living. However, she knew that his favorite band was the Electric Light Orchestra. Hockey was a sport that she would not tackle, but she could handle music. She was now the proud owner of every recording that ELO ever created, thought about, or laid down on CD, tape, or vinyl, and she had to admit that the music was very cool. Even if this day was a flop, at least she had a new favorite band. She knew every song, every album release and every detail of the band, and her cell phone had every MP3 recoding of ELO loaded on it now. She even knew the name of the street in Birmingham, England, where Jeff Lynne grew up. The encyclopedia-like knowledge of ELO would be the icebreaker. After all, she had some English blood in her veins.

She was no English Rose, but today was the day.

A short drive in her car, a final check of her makeup, a confident walk into the restaurant and an adjustment to the light inside as opposed to the outside light. There he was at the bar in his favorite bar stool, and today, he was looking better than the laws of human attraction should allow. Faint be her heart because the gods smiled upon her . . . the seat next to him was open.

"Hi, is this seat taken?" Her question floated in the air while she allowed the dangle of hair across her face. Her enchanting eyes flickered while asking the question. He finished a sip of his beer, smiled that killer smile, and his golden voice riveted her soul.

With a wave in the direction of the bar stool, the words floated in the air, "No. Please. Sit. Enjoy."

She swore that out of the corner of his eyes; he watched her settle into the bar stool and there were smiles all around.

Damn, she wished that her jeans were not so tight.

The bartender smiled with a rather phony smile laced with a touch of jealousy and greeted her, and the bartender's smile told the story that she knew the plan.

The bartender winked, nodded, and took her drink order. She looked down as her cell phone blinked and beeped with a text.

It was a text from the bartender and it read, "**Good luck. I never have had any. May the best girl win.**"

Two Mimosas later and the silence remained. He had not said another word and her palms were sweaty and she was feeling a little loose and loopy. Time to make a move. Time for a third Mimosa. A girl needs her courage. Liquid or otherwise.

Today was the day. Convinced that small talk would not cut it, she went for the brass ring. She opened her purse, pulled out her earbuds and placed them in her ears. God gave her a gift, and that was her singing voice. Well, God also gave her some very nice female curves, a pretty face, and other attributes, but to this man, she was sure that meant little. When you looked like he did, women threw those gifts at him right and left.

With a flick of the screen, she dialed up *Out of the Blue*, scrolled to *It's Over* and waltzed in for the kill. While pretending to glance at the menus to pick out some food, in order to absorb the alcohol taking over her mind and body, off she went into the opening words.

Not a loud singing voice, not an obnoxious singing voice, but just loud enough, "Summer came and passed away. . .." His head swung around and he smiled.

Pay dirt smelled so sweet. As if, it was fresh-turned dirt in a spring garden.

"It's over, it's over. . .."

Another smile and some words as he stared at her.

"Electric Light Orchestra, huh? I would not think they were your style," he said with a knockout smile and a wave of his hands. It took all that she could muster up to pretend that she was only slightly paying attention.

While taking the earbuds out of her ears, she asked, "Say again. I did not hear you. I am sorry."

"No, my apologies for bothering you. I said, ELO. I did not figure you to be an ELO type of woman. I am a huge fan of ELO. Huge."

"Oh, cool. That is a coincidence. I love them too," she said with one of the best acting jobs this side of Hollywood.

He paused and then waved at her with her hand. It had to be a New Jersey thing. She found it very appealing.

"I have seen you in here before . . . but there is something different. Maybe your hair?"

"Well, yes, it is a new style. I was not too sure about it. And yes, I love ELO. Out of the Blue is amazing."

Once more, he studied her and her heart went pitter-patter and boom, boom, and a final, resounding BOOM! He gently reached up, pushed the dangle of hair out of her face, and tucked it gently behind her ear.

"I needed to move that hair to see your face better. You are stunning, please, be sure about it. You look gorgeous. Say, let me buy your drinks there. And lunch too."

The words were almost a sputter, "Well, okay. Thank you. . .."

"What is your favorite ELO song? I am kind of partial to, It's Over, and appears if you are too."

Two hours later, he had invited her to an Electric Light Orchestra reunion concert in Philadelphia, scheduled for about two months from now. Two months! Oh my! He said that he had extra tickets. She missed the Philadelphia date in her research, and she honestly had no idea they were even touring again. Wow, thank you, God! Oh yes, and he invited her to dinner for later that evening. He paid their tabs; they slipped off the bar stools and headed for the door together.

Yes, today was the day.

Her cell phone blinked and beeped and with a smile, she looked over at the bartender who had sent a simple text, **"Wow! How did u pull that off?!!!**

She paused and texted back, **"I had a secret weapon. Mr. Blue Sky. Google it."**

Yes, her jeans were tight now.

Yet, she had a feeling that in a little while they were going to become much looser.

A Gift. Freely Given

From: Flashes, Sparks, and Shorts: Flash One

On the first day, the drill instructor told us that some of us might die. It was a risk that I knew I needed to accept. Honestly, I never thought it would happen to me. I never really did.

I was wrong.

One of my brothers in arms holds my hand. Tightly. He tells me to hang on. He tugs at my body armor. I cannot really see him. Everything is a blur.

There is no pain. There was for a second, but now it is gone.

A Navy Corpsman works on me. He shouts something. It is hopeless. I feel my life fading.

It will be all right. I knew the risk. I signed up for this. I am a volunteer.

The sun fades. I see my lover. I see her lovely face. I feel our passion. I see our daughter. I will never see her grow up. I will never see her laugh, smile, or dance.

I see my mother, my father, and my sister. My best friend. They will cry. They will miss me. They will stand by and weep as they lower me into the cold ground. They will fly the American flag from their porches.

It will fly free and it will fly proud.

It will be all right. I knew the risk. I never thought it would happen to me. I was wrong. Some Marines must pay the price. There have been many before me and there will be many after me. Those who are willing. Where others choose to hide and to pretend.

Damn, I am only twenty-two years old. That is how it goes. I did this for you. And for him and for her and for them. I don't even know your names. I never will. Please never waste this effort. This life.

I gave you this gift, and it was free. It is my life. My commitment to you and yours. So that you could live, free. To do as you please. As you choose to do.

I knew the risk. No one made me sign up for this. Everyone must die. My time is now here.

Remember.

Yet, as I lay dying and bleeding—I only wish for one thing. That you know that I did this for you and yours and for them. I did this, not for any specific skin color, or a man, or a woman, or for any race, or for any religion.

For you.

It is a gift. Freely given.

It is my life.

Around Eight O'clock

From: Flashes, Sparks, and Shorts: Flash One

It was Saturday morning, around eight o'clock. He knew that his girlfriend's father was off to work already. He worked every Saturday and Wednesday was his day off.

The summer was almost over. You could feel the change of the seasons in the air. Especially so in the early morning. When the dew sets hard. When the moisture invades the grass all the way down to the roots where the plants touch the soil.

He could see his warm breath hit the air in puffs. Gentle puffs while he wiped the dew off his prized Camaro. The car of his dreams, preparing to ride to change his life and her life and ride off to God only knows with the woman of his dreams. Perhaps.

The air temperature would warm up later, maybe by the time they hit Interstate Eighty. They could roll down the windows. Perhaps.

All the clothes he owned and the few possessions that he claimed in his entire life of twenty-three years sat in the trunk of the Camaro. The clothes fit in one small bag and the possessions hardly took up half the trunk. In his wallet, he had his life savings. One-thousand-twenty-seven dollars. Along with pocket change. His one suit, as his dear mother called it, "His Sunday or Funeral suit" hung on a hanger in the back seat. On the hook. If his gal agreed to his plan, there was more than enough room for her clothes and belongings.

Women usually had more clothes and belongings than men did.

When he tossed the wiping rag into the trunk and slammed the lid down, he thought, 'Hell, anyone had more stuff than I do.'

That fact did not bother him in the least. In fact, it made it much easier for this plan to take place.

He climbed into the Camaro, fired off the LT1, and the engine roared to life with a deep power that always set his blood flowing throughout his entire body. Just as she did when she smiled at him and when they made love. Other men would look at his gal and think that she was not a bombshell, but to him she was the entire universe. He loved the way her hair fell all around him when they locked in an embrace, and the way sweat appeared on her upper lips when they loved so deep and so powerfully. The flash of her dark eyes followed by a sigh and a smile.

The clutch hit the floor, and the gearshift set hard into first gear after a quick jaunt in reverse. He stopped in the turnaround and stared at the house. His uncle and aunt were good people. The best. They took him in when his parents left this world, and he owed them a huge debt of gratitude. His uncle understood the need to leave; however, his aunt not so much. The discussion last night was difficult. He would miss them, and his cousins were very cool.

Christmas and Thanksgiving were for visiting.

The tires spun, and the engine roared. He heard and felt some rocks kick up from under the tires. He knew his aunt was behind the curtain peeking out at the scene with tears in her eyes and his uncle had his hand on her back in support and comfort. That was the kind of love he wished for with his woman and damn well, if he was not off to claim it.

There was nothing left here for him. For them. It was a tired old Jersey Shore town. Old and tired.

It was a short drive to her house. They grew up together in this little Jersey Shore town. Fell in love in the third grade.

The Camaro spun its tires again when he hit the edge of his girlfriend's driveway. Every time, he downshifted and then popped the clutch a little. LT1 power. Old-school Detroit. He was sure the roar of the engine alerted everyone in his woman's house that he arrived. This visit was unscheduled. No one knew he was coming over today. Not this early. Not even his girlfriend. Especially not her.

There she was on the porch; her dress wisped around her ankles. The sun shone all around her body and he smiled and held his breath as he pushed in the clutch, shifted to first gear, and quieted the roar of the LT1. Then he moved the ignition key to the accessory position, pushed in the tape, dialed up the song and turned up the volume. His woman stood with her hands on her hips and shrugged her shoulders.

"Do Ya? Do ya? Do, ya, do ya, want my love?" Jeff sang one of their favorite songs as he jumped out of the Camera and without saying a word; he ran to the trunk, used his trunk key, and popped it open. He pulled out the bag, held it in the air, and smiled as Jeff continued to ask the same question with that mean-ass guitar lick.

Now, she grew concerned as she realized their dreams were suddenly reality before her eyes. Those dreamy discussions after making love in the back seat of the Camaro were no longer so dreamy.

Her mother appeared on the porch. She held the screen

door gently open, and then she carefully let it close without a noise. His brother must still be sleeping. Her mother wiped her hands on the dishtowel she held in her hands and then tucked it into her apron. Concern washed over her face as she realized the situation.

His throat closed; he did not waver in holding the bag in the air.

He thought, 'Now or never, baby.'

Yet, he spoke not a single word. Some scenes in life require no words. His gal only stood and studied him for what was only seconds or perhaps a minute, but seemed as if it were ten lifetimes. Or more.

Suddenly, she turned and spun on her heels. Once more, her dress wisped at her ankles and she pulled the door open and darted inside the house. Her mother glanced quickly in his direction; their eyes met briefly, before spinning on her heels and following her daughter into the home. This time no one held open the door. If he had to bet, her brother was now awake.

Slowly, he lowered the bag and held it at his side as he peered at the porch. His throat remained closed and even a swallow did not clear it. He thought this would be easier with her father gone and at work. Perhaps.

Lives in the balance.

"Where are we going?" She asked as she rolled down the window and the wind from Interstate 80 rushed in and blew her hair all around her face. She pushed her hair away from in front of her face as she turned to face him and study him, as he remained focused down the road.

"Somewhere out there," he said while waving with one hand at the windshield. "We will let our hearts tell us when to stop. I mean, does it really matter?"

"No, no," she shook her head and smiled while staring

out the window and pushing her hair away again from her face, "not really. As long as we are together. That is all that really matters."

It was Saturday morning. Around eleven o'clock now.

The LT1 purred like a kitten.

Long Legs, Wine, and Beer

From: Flashes, Sparks, and Shorts: Flash One

It was a hot summer night. You needed to stay hydrated. It was hot, and then it grew even hotter.

When you are a world-famous rock-and-roll superstar, you can have your pick of the women. Young or old, and all of them in between. They flock to you as if you are God's gift to everything. Groupies surround concerts and the after-concert parties like moths to a flame. Except this young woman was not a groupie.

She was anything but a groupie.

To establish a point and in order to clarify the situation and amplify the story, she was only there to do her job. World-famous rock-and-roll-superstars meant nothing to her.

Despite the best efforts of the front man of the rock-and-roll band to attract her attention, she only smiled and went diligently back to her work.

Her use of the English language was not the best; the band member's proficiency of the Hungarian language was even worse, but even with the language barriers, it was painfully obvious that all that this beautiful woman wanted to do was her job and then she would be on her way. There was just a whisper in the broken communication of her being an athlete. You did not need to be a top-notch detective to determine that fact.

Her glorious body confirmed that fact. Her legs were

long with a hint of power and muscles. Her hips were slender. Her breasts . . . perfect. Her smile captivating. Her backside . . . perfect.

Then there were her legs. Long legs.

Seemingly endless, in fact. They went on forever and then some more.

Her primary job was to cater the musical event. Before the concert, it was beer, wine, water, and some sandwiches and snacks. Into a cooler and onto a table in the back-of-the-house.

Her inadvertent job was to enthrall the band members and tune up their lust to immeasurable levels. Particularly, the lead front man of the band. His eyes nearly popped out of his head, and it was difficult for him to remain focused upon the looming concert.

A concert that was just a short time away.

Enter stage right. Or left.

When she bent down to load the cooler with the beer bottles, the wine and the water, every man within twenty miles held their breath. Tight shorts, black, silky hair that fell all around her as she worked and that required her to tuck behind her ears, tanned and long legs, a hint of her cotton panties and a whisper of what glory lies underneath the covers.

Her beauty could peel the paint from the walls of the old music house. It sent shivers down the lead front man's spine and made his legs shake.

Yet, all she did was smile at the playful inquires and suggestions embedded within the conversation of the band members and deflect the lust and wave with her delicate, yet powerful hands and dismiss them. The language barrier was easy to hide behind in the process of deflection. Perhaps she understood much more of the language than she pretended to understand.

Perhaps.

It worked for her and did not work for them.

It was obvious that she had a man in her life. A lover. A husband. A lucky man. Very lucky.

The concert went off without a hitch. Perfect. Despite the heat.

The heat of the day and the heat, back stage.

The lead front man thought of her when he sang the love songs. When he performed the ballads. Her vision and impact made a difference. The songs were poignant, honest, and sincere.

Tomorrow, the music critics would rave about the concert performance. Particularly of the performance and abilities of the lead front man for the band. All while not knowing or even remotely imagining the inspiration behind them all.

If only they did. Perhaps, they too, would be rock-and-roll superstars.

Perhaps.

After the concert, in the back of the house, there was no sign of her. Her job was now complete. The sandwiches, snacks and wine and beer were all perfect.

As was she.

The front man went to dinner the next night before they left out of town. To head west. On with the next stop on the tour.

He imagined that every female in the restaurant was she. The greeter, the server, the woman sitting next to him, who laughed too much.

For a second, he thought one of the servers might be

her. Did she work a part-time job here? His eyes peered intently in and he studied the woman from afar. Simply a trick of his imagination. It was dreaming on his part.

Sadly, she was not there. Forever, she might haunt him. That was okay; because he would use her as a muse to write songs and elevate his stardom.

Honestly, he would rather have her.

In his arms. In his heart.

Forever.

It was a hot summer night. You needed to stay hydrated. It was hot, and then it grew a bit colder. A cool and welcoming breeze settled in when they arrived at the hotel.

A gentle breeze with a whisper of autumn upon its waves.

The desk clerk had a pleasant smile, but she could not hold a candle to her.

No other woman could ever do so.

Forever.

The Drill Instructor

From: Flashes, Sparks, and Shorts: Flash One

"Mens! I will tell you here and now that some of you standing here right now, will die! Yes, you will die! No sense in sugarcoating shit. Because, guess what? It will still be shit. No, I am not God, so I cannot tell you when or how, some of you will die, but I know this to be true. In my twenty or so years of teaching and training patsy-asses like all of you losers are right now, to become Marines, I have learned from experience that Marines die. Some of you might die in combat, with a bullet clean through your head. A clean kill contains elements of honor when you are in battle. Others might tumble on your sorry asses, and be run over by a truck and have all your guts pushed outta of ya! Others will succumb to some rare-ass disease, but what you have to understand is that you will die in service to your beloved Marine Corps and to your country. To die as a warrior, as a United States Marine, is an honor. It is not as if you are dying, no, no no, Mens, it is as if you are promoted to a higher mission!"

While he bellowed at the top of his voice, the drill instructor slowly walked back and forth in front of his new recruits. It was the first few hours of the critical first meeting, the first day of basic training. His highly polished shoes glistened in the sun, his uniform, despite the heat, remained crisp and fresh. If you looked closely, you could see hints of beads of sweat working their way down the sides of his temples.

Despite the popular opinion of the multitudes, drill

instructors are human. They do sweat. However, the drops of sweat contain salt, honor, and courage.

The drill instructor stopped pacing and with one arm, and his hand outstretched to Heaven, he dramatically pointed in the air to the American flag waving on the pole high above his head.

His previously bellowing voice softened and lowered. The drill instructor grew solemn.

It almost seemed impossible for him to do so, but he did lower his booming voice as he explained, "For that flag, to wave in the breeze, above our heads, and for it to fly as freely as it does, unencumbered, proud, strong, it took a damn lot of blood and guts. Mens, the expectations of those who shed their blood and their guts, is that there would be many to follow in their footsteps. You will not let them down, nor let your beloved United States Marine Corps down, your country down, or God down. I know in my heart that is true, so help me God."

The drill instructor turned and faced the front and center of the formation of want-to-be-Marines, he stood tall and proud in front of the nervous recruits, he tucked his arms at his side and his face was stoic, yet proud. He lowered his head so that you could just see the top of his eyes ominously peering out from under the edge of his drill instructor's hat.

Once again, he spoke in a somber tone, "Mens, be forewarned . . . I know in my heart that this is true and if I fail in my mission, if I fail that flag, fail my beloved Marine Corps and fail those who have shed their blood and their guts . . . then, I will gladly pay the price of having done so."

The Old Apple Tree and the Young Boy with the Limp

From: Flashes, Sparks, and Shorts: Flash One

Children can be so cruel to one another.

"It happens. Disease damages. It is no one's fault. His right leg will always be a little shorter than his left leg is."

The baby's parents stared in at the doctor with intense concern upon their faces. The doctor sensed the concern, and he performed a quick layer of damage control with his ensuing words to relieve their concerns.

"Look," the good doctor said with an air of sympathy within his voice, "he will never be a sprinting champion, or a soccer star, or an athlete of any kind, but aside from his limp, with some intense rehabilitation work, I am quite sure that he will lead a normal life. Maybe, even, do extraordinary things."

The father looked up at the doctor with a deep sadness in his eyes. Often, deep stares from human eyes are so telling in their meaning.

"Thank you, doctor. Ah, rehabilitation? We are simple farmers. We own several apple orchards. Money is tight. To say the least. It always will be. Nothing much changes when you are a farmer. Yet, our trees have stories to tell, and to hear, and much love to give. Please, tell me, how much does intense rehabilitation cost?"

The doctor sighed.

"Ha, ha, ha! Old short leg has no friends! All he has is

his stupid books. He always walks around with his head down and his eyes glued to the pages of stupid books," the evil bully said to the young boy with the limp as a squeeze of disgusting foamy spittle edged out of the corners of his mouth. Bullies are ugly in so many ways. If their mothers could only see them now.

"I have friends! More friends than you do," the young boy with the limp, protested his response to the bully.

"You do? Who? Crusoe, Scrooge, Holmes and Watson? Dickens? Ha! Characters in your dusty old books do not count as actual friends."

The young boy with the limp hung his head and sadly walked away with his books tucked under his arm.

"We will need to level the north quadrant come the spring of next year," the farmer said to his helper as they shared a few beers together on a cold winter's night and planned the farming for the next year. "As soon as the snow melts, we will pull 'em out, cut 'em down and sell the apple wood. They are under producers. Especially the big, old one in the first row. Only a few quality fruits last year. Shame, cuz, used it to be a helluva tree. Just too old now, I 'magine. Disease must'a damaged it now."

The helper nodded. He made a note in his pad and took a sip of beer when he finished scribbling with his pencil.

When you are a farmer, the winter was for planning.

Hearing the words, the young boy with the limp picked his head out of the book he was reading and he carefully listened to his father's words.

A single tear ran down his cheek. He loved the pinks and whites of apple blossoms in the spring.

Disease damaged it.

It was bitterly cold. January can tear at you and chill at

you and bite at you as none other of the twelve months can.

Undaunted from the bite of the cold, the young boy with the limp walked through the crusty snow. He stopped in front of the old tree, and he studied it. The big old one in the first row. The young boy with the limp knew that tree was the leader for the rest of the trees. He could feel it because the young boy with the limp could do extraordinary things.

The twisty branches reached toward Heaven and beyond. They were dormant in the cold and sleeping until the warmth awoke them. Yet, the young boy with the limp knew that they could hear his words and feel his love.

Love can warm the coldest day, dispel the harshest wind, and echo all the way to Heaven.

He sat down in the snow at the base of the tree and opened his book.

The first words that he read from the first dusty, old book were loud and clear, "I think that I shall never see. A poem as lovely as a tree. A tree whose. . .."

Every day, the young boy with the limp arrived, and every day, he read his books aloud at the base of the big, old apple tree that was the first in the row.

Adventures of Holmes, the healed bitterness of Scrooge and the trickery of the dodger.

The young boy with the limp had many friends.

Spring arrived, and the snow melted. Rebirth of the previous latent and interesting dormancy arrived too. Warmth and sun, and birds and soft breezes that caused the snow to run away into the edges of the orchard.

"Well, faint be my heart," the farmer said as he gazed at the extraordinary display of stunning apple blossoms perched on countless twisty branches framed in a clear blue sky. Branches that reached to Heaven and beyond. Pinks and white and gentle pistils waved to the old farmer in the lovely spring breeze. Welcoming his gaze, loving his thoughts, and embracing his care. It took his breath away.

"Fooled me. I guess that old tree recovered and lookie at that. So did the rest of the trees in the row, too. Gonna be an exceptional year."

The farmer's helper nodded and scribbled in his notepad as he crossed off his notes from last winter.

The glorious apple trees in the old apple orchard had stories to tell, and to hear, and much love to give.

As did the young boy with the limp.

As do we all.

The Puzzle

From: Flashes, Sparks, and Shorts: Flash Two

"Well, you said that you wanted to see yourself as others do. Or better yet, to see inside of your own soul past your thoughts and even past your body," the husband said to his wife.

His wife nodded. She looked up and smiled a forced and weak smile.

"Please, I appreciate your idea and the suggestion and I am not belittling it, but right now, with all my troubles, it seems sort of a simple, yet silly thing to do. I mean, how can it help? I am struggling with everything. To feel what I used to feel. To handle and control my emotions. To function somewhat normally. We have tried so much. Endured it all. Medications, doctors, and analysts, and even hypnotists, it goes on and on too long now. Depression destroyed my soul and my life. Our lives. I feel so worthless."

Her breath hitched, and the words stumbled out of her mouth.

"I love you so much," her eyes were sad while she spoke the words. The wife looked down and then up again and studied his face.

The concern washed over him, but he did not speak a single word.

"I am so sorry for what I put you through for all of these years. You are a good man and a better husband than I deserve."

He shook his head and lifted his whiskey glass. He swirled the brown liquor around so it washed the sides of the glass. His eyes studied the liquor as it settled into the mixture. Licks of whiskey remained on the glass as he held it steady, and then it oozed down the side and the whiskey all joined in unison. The husband took a sip. A long sip and then he set the glass down.

Two fingers left in the glass.

"No, sorry, ever. Ever, ever, ever. Honey, I love you and need to do better for you. You are a rare and precious woman. Let's try it. What can it hurt? As a photographer, I capture images of the world, of people, of life and retain them forever. The beauty of it all. The art, the fleeting seconds of a moment of time that I capture forever. It gives me such honor to do so. It is a broken puzzle of the images through my lens that I assemble together into a glorious photograph. Furthermore, I can say that as a writer, I remove parts and pieces of my soul in my words, in my stories, in my thoughts. I expose every aspect of my soul to the reader. Then, when I finally finish assembling the multitude of words, I put the parts and pieces of my soul back together and feel whole once more. I feel renewed. I feel amazing when I finish the last words of a book or story. I am whole."

He took another sip.

One finger left and his eyes went to the bottle sitting on the kitchen counter.

"Okay, let's try it. After all, it is only . . . what . . . maybe thirty dollars to have the company make it? If it helps me feel better, even for just a moment, then it is priceless."

He smiled and nodded.

Nothing felt right. She seemed so tense. The photos were

not an accurate picture of her. He was a damn talented photographer but no matter what pose, what facial expression, or what approach he took to the subject, or what suggestion he offered; he could not take the picture that he needed. The flow was all wrong. He snapped and snapped, and then after viewing the last photograph on the screen, the husband sighed.

"What's wrong?" The wife asked.

"Maybe you need to see you as I see you."

"I don't understand. Here I am. Right in front of you. You must have taken over a hundred pictures."

"No, as I see you when we share our love. Naked. Exposed. Your body and soul bare. Unfettered. You are beautiful. We all need to open our souls to understand our complexities. We cannot hide in shells. Skin is just a shell of protection that conceals our true identity. You need to see past your body. See the magnificence underneath. The true you. The woman that I adore. With all my heart and soul. You need to see my love. The source of it. Us. One love. One person."

She nodded and stripped. Her clothes fell into a pile at her feet.

She relaxed.

He took a deep breath as he studied her through the lens of the camera. This was perfect! She was stunning. Even more so than she was thirty years ago when they first met and fell in love.

He aimed and snapped off the pictures.

They sent the best one of the ten photos off to the company.

It arrived two weeks later.

In a black box. Thirty-six dollars with the shipping costs.

Three fingers in his glass. A half-full glass of red wine for his wife. The lights in the room were dim. A scented candle flickered on the table. It had a captivating autumn scent to it. A woodsy scent.

They set the mood.

She laughed as the pieces fell out of the box and tumbled onto the dining room table.

"There are so many pieces of me!" The wife exclaimed.

"Well, we requested a five-hundred piece you. Looks as if we have it too."

"Okay, so will, you help?" The wife asked as a dangle of black hair fell in front of her face.

"No, honey, you have to do it alone. You have to make yourself whole. I will watch." He spoke the words, reached over and pushed the dangle of hair away and gently tucked it behind her ear.

Two fingers, then one.

Empty wine glass. Refills all around.

The clock ticked onward and there were more refills and some laughs.

One finger left and five pieces too.

They all fit perfectly. The last one was on her right leg. It was a tricky one. A daunting task completed. It took a few hours and some wine and some whiskey and some hard work and deep thinking. Some test fits, no, actually, thousands of test fits. Spinning the pieces in the air, gliding over the others, so many pieces, studying them, placing them here and there and everywhere. It was so difficult to see it all. Yet, it was her! Her own naked self. Exposed, open, right in front of her. How could it be so difficult to know your own self? Some of the pieces seemed nearly impossible to make them fit. Frustrating. Complex.

Nevertheless, she made it all work. It all fit. The wife did it alone, without any help at all from the husband. Because she had to do it alone. It was the only way to heal.

She was broken into five-hundred pieces. Complex, twisting, with smooth and jagged edges that all fit together into one amazing picture. One beautiful picture.

We are all intricate, we all have smooth edges and difficult edges and turns and twists. Some of us are made up of two-hundred pieces, some of us are made of thousands, some of us are made of millions. Some of our pieces are large and others are small. Some are easy to find and fit together, and others seem nearly impossible. Eventually, even if we are broken, we all need to make the pieces fit. We need to be whole. All of us are a puzzle.

The ultimate puzzle.

The wife leaned back, and she giggled, and then she smiled widely. She took a sip of wine and nodded for her husband to lift his whiskey glass. She felt that a toast was in order. Their glasses made a gentle "clink" as they touched. They both studied the glory of the picture in front of them on the table. She was gorgeous. She was whole.

No longer did she see that her breasts were not as perky as they once were, or that her belly had some extra skin and was no longer taut, or that her legs were too fat near the hips. All she saw was her, she, the wife, the lover, the mother, the woman, the glow of her love, and most of all she saw the stunning beauty of her inner soul.

Tears filled her eyes and her husband placed his arm around her shoulders and pulled her in tight to his body. To his warmth. To his love.

"Is this how you see me?"

He nodded and smiled. A few tears licked the edges of his eyes.

"I *am* gorgeous. I am *not* worthless. Maybe, I am even priceless. Oh, my love . . . I see what you see now."

"Yes! I told you. Now, maybe, you can believe me and believe in you too. To realize how rare and precious that you are. To me, to our children, and to this world, and to God."

She nodded and whispered, while the tears streamed down her cheeks, "I am whole again. I was broken and now I am whole. I do love you with all my heart and soul. You are so wonderful. I feel how you feel when you finish a story or a book. Or when you see a viewer's eyes widen when they study one of your photographs. It must feel glorious to you when you write the last word. I understand now. It is all so amazing."

He wiped away her tears. He gently used his fingers. Then he took his own tears away.

One-by-one.

No tears remained.

She said no more words, but she reached out and took him by his hand and she gently lifted him off the chair.

In silence, they made their way to the stairs. To their bedroom. No words or conversation required.

Their love followed along.

On the way, the husband blew out the candle.

The smoke from the dying flame slowly drifted into the air.

You could smell the remnants of the smoke while it purified the air, as only a dying flame can do.

Then he shut off the lights.

The puzzle glowed in the darkness. Next to the glasses.

One finger left in the whiskey glass.

No wine remained.

Old Patty's Magic Mixture

From: Flashes, Sparks, and Shorts: Flash Two

We often overlook parsnips in our gardens and at the markets and we miss their magical flavor and power. Parsnips aren't the most attractive of the vegetables; but they have some hidden magic and have a distinct flavor. Yet, they are obscure. Never overlook the obscure things in life. Dig deep because beneath the surface of our visible world, the best things lie in wait for us to enjoy.

Jobs were hard to find and times were tough.

"Here is all that I got tonight, Old Patty. Sorry. We were busy today. Christmas Eve, ya know. These blue-bloods got dough to spend. They never suffer much. Not much leftovers in here," the prep chef for the fancy restaurant on Main Street said as he set a pot of leftover food on the rear stoop in the snow.

Old Patty shuffled over to it, bent down, and stared into the pot. Carrots, asparagus, some small pieces of chicken bits, chicken bones, assorted other veggies such as sections of squash, some onion pieces, and parsnips.

"Thanks, Oscar. It is fine. I can certainly work with this. Especially the parsnips. A Christmas feast for us. Do ya have any spare salt?"

Oscar nodded, disappeared, and reappeared with a few packets of salt.

"Here. Merry Christmas, Old Patty. If ya can dry up, I would love to have ya back."

Old Patty shrugged his shoulders, picked up the pot and said, "Maybe. Not now. What for? I enjoy the hooch too much and I would not show up for days and let ya down. Merry Christmas. I will bring the pot back and leave it here. Washed and spotless."

It was 1976 and times were tough in old Paterson, New Jersey. In Hawthorne, in Haledon and in Totowa Borough too. All over. Jobs turned to dust.

Christmas Eve brought heavy snow, ice, cold, and no joy this year.

Morris worked in a machine shop until they closed it, Teddy was a printer for the local newspaper, until they sent his job to Pennsylvania, and Ross had not worked in years. No one ever knew what Ross did for a living.

Old Patty McGrath was a cook in the Navy. He worked as a cook and a chef for many years in various restaurants until his wife left, and the bottle became his best friend. Patty blamed his heritage for his love of whiskey.

Partly true. Mostly false.

Everyone had a story during these dark days.

The holes in their hearts matched the darkness of the days.

The snowfall was good for a few bucks. They shoveled snow all day and had some cash. The group spent most of the dough on cheap whiskey and wine. A little dabble of Christmas cheer.

None of them had a home these days. Unless the maintenance shed at the railway yard just off the turn on East Railway Avenue counted as a home. The lead maintenance mechanic for the railroad looked the other way and often left the door unlocked. Especially on the wintry nights. The group left a few bucks for the lead maintenance mechanic to pay him off for the "home."

In New Jersey, side dough and pay-offs were a way of life.

The night watchman looked the other way, too. He took the five bucks and considered it a Christmas tip. After all, the small group never stole anything or caused any troubles.

The fire was enormous. Old pallets worked well as fuel. They stacked a steel barrel up on cement blocks salvaged from the side of the rail tracks. The snow lay deep in the yard and the night grew colder and colder. Intense.

Warm puffs of breath rose in the air as Morris, Teddy, and Ross huddled around the fire, sipped the Christmas cheer, and told stories of better days. What they could remember of them.

While they sipped and spoke, they watched Old Patty prepare their Christmas Eve feast.

Old Patty melted clean snow; first, he steamed the heaping mixture of all the veggies minus the parsnips through an old window screen perched across the top of the pot and hung over the barrel's flames.

"Don't worry, I washed it!" Old Patty dispelled any worries on his barrel-cooking-hygiene measures. "Gotta steam 'em to clean 'em, and besides, I need the steamed-off broth."

Old Patty carefully captured the broth and added the salt. He chopped the parsnips up into very fine bits with his pocket knife. The broth went into the pot along with the chicken bits and the bones. Finally, into the pot went the parsnips. Then over the hot barrel, the pot went.

Old Patty sifted the bones through the screen and carefully poured each of his friends a steaming mug of the soup.

They found some old coffee mugs in the maintenance

shed, and they worked well for soup bowls. Some spoons too. They would wash them and return them, too.

"The parsnips are the key ingredient in the mixture here, youse guys. Distinct flavor," Old Patty explained as he took a long sip of whiskey and wobbled over to the pot. His eyes peered into the boiling mixture and he stirred the remaining soup and smiled. It smelled incredible.

"Wow! Merry Christmas, Old Patty. Thanks! This soup is fantastic. It might be the best thing that I ate all year," Morris excitedly exclaimed as he dished the soup out of the coffee mug.

"Yes, fantastic! I will sleep well with a full belly tonight," Teddy commented.

Ross agreed with a nod. Ross said little these days.

"And that rot-gut whiskey in your veins will help ya sleep too, Teddy. Thank you. If I dare say, it is quite good. My best mixture ever," Old Patty said, as he tasted his soup and peered into the flames.

"Yup. The best I ever made. Merry Christmas."

"What are ya gonna call it?" Morris asked.

"Old Patty's Magic Mixture. Gonna leave some for Oscar to try when I return the pot. I found a jar, and I bet he would really enjoy it."

"My goodness, Old Patty! That soup was incredible. I asked the new owner to try it and he flipped over it. He wants ya to come back. Says he will put it on the menu. Can ya duplicate it? Do ya 'member the recipe?" Oscar asked as he excitedly explained the results of tasting the magic mixture.

"Of course, I can duplicate it. Oscar, the parsnips are the key. They have a very distinct taste."

"The V-A has programs to dry ya out. C'mon, Old Patty.

Ya served our country. Now, let them pay ya back a little. The owner said he could help ya out and work with ya. Please."

"Well, maybe. I will think about it. Thanks."

"Honey, be sure when you go to the Foodworld to pick up a few more cans of that amazing soup you bought last week. What's it called? That fancy veggie chicken soup."

"Oh yes, Old Patty's Magic Mixture. Super delicious and a very cool label logo too. I love the steel barrel in the railroad yard logo with the hobos standing around the fire making the soup. I will look for some cans. The store always sells out so quickly, though."

That next Christmas Eve, the lead maintenance mechanic did not have to leave the maintenance-shed door unlocked. The night watchman did not pick up an extra five bucks, either.

The parsnips were the key.

The Dream

From: Flashes, Sparks, and Shorts: Flash Two

Other than the woman he currently sat with, he did not have many, if any, friends around him these days. In fact, on any other days, too. He was a loner. A composer of words, and of books, and he kept occupied in his spare time with assorted dabbling of sentences and of those same words. He danced between lines and flirted with the meaning of his words. When he did not dance, he captured life, people, and adventures in photos while staring through his camera lens. I guess you could say that he was a writer, a photographer, and a loner.

It had not always been that way. Years ago, he had so much more, but he hid the words and the images within his spirit to pick the proper time to reveal them when the time was right to do so. When the time came to release the parts and pieces of his own soul to the world and to find his purpose. Yet, then, in that time and place, which seemed so long ago now, he had love surrounding him and somehow, because of circumstances and the fact that he returned love harder than he valued his own soul, he did what he thought was best for those he loved.

Now he was alone with his words, his images, and his ghosts of the past and the dreams.

She was a special friend. She cared deeply for him, and he cared deeply for her. A special bond of kindred spirits. He was complex, and he had the type of aura around him, where you wanted to stare at it and wonder what was going on so deep inside of his mind and soul.

They shared a connection. Working together and being together for many years had made them intuitive of each other.

She had deep and beautiful dark brown eyes where a man could get lost in them for a very long time. Maybe forever.

He had magical eyes, and she often got lost in his too. Forever.

It had been a particularly wearisome day.

Their exhausted souls gathered for a break. The COVID-19 crisis wore them down; yet, they plowed onward and did their best to get by. It seemed as the entire world was crazy and they were the only ones holding it together on their end.

They shared a sugary snack, and she broke it into even halves. He leaned back and nodded, took the snack, and took a small bite. Sugary snacks were not his favorite, but today was an awful day and the sugar rush might overcome some of the pain and the weariness.

After a bite, a chew, and a swallow, he sighed, and she studied his face. Her sense of his pain absorbed into her. His weariness was telling. It was unusual for him. He usually had limitless energy.

His mind raced with thoughts of the past fifteen years or thereabouts. The long, long journey that brought him to where he was now. With her. In the here, and in the there, and in the now.

His words came out, "I often think that I will suddenly wake up from a dream. I will be sitting in my backyard, on my patio, in a lawn chair, at my house in New Hampshire, a beer or whiskey flask in my hand. I will still be wearing a suit and tie from driving from New Jersey to New

Hampshire after my last week at my long-time job ended and snow will be piling up on top of my head. I will open my eyes, blink, look around and say aloud, 'Wow, that was some amazing dream. I ended up in Virginia after a long journey that included so many experiences. I met so many people. Some nice. Most not too nice. I traveled all over the country. Lived in Atlanta, Georgia for a few years and then lived on the road in hotels across the country. It was amazing. From California to Florida and all states in between. So many wild and crazy things. So much pain. Some happiness. Some wonderful experiences and some awful ones. Tremendous loneliness. I will say, 'What a crazy dream.' I will stand up, stretch, look around, and clean the snow off my head and with my drink in my hand walk back into the house."

She studied his face, and it was then that he knew that his profound thoughts had penetrated her. She too became lost in a potential dream of her past life or lives.

"Would you wake up? Do you wake up? Knowing what you know now, the experiences, the many stories written, the photographs taken, the people you met, do you indeed wake up in New Hampshire? None of this ever having happened and losing every memory of it all? Of the books, the photos, and the words, the hard work, the pain, of me, of you, of everything. Do you wake up?"

Her questions were profound, but exact, and given what they two of them shared together and the hard work and dedication that brought them to where we were right now, and facing the loss of what they stood to lose, it was spine-tingling.

He leaned back and thought deeply before answering.

Tears rimmed her eyes as she wandered in her own dream, posed the same questions to herself, and it nearly tore them both apart.

Past adventures, past pain, a past that she, too, ran away from a long time ago, somewhere in a dream.

Dreams that always remain and dreams from which the two of them never awake.

The answer was simple. On the other hand, was it?

He looked over at his partner in sugary delight and he felt her love. She felt his love too. It was powerful. It remained a dutiful romance, and a genuine friendship.

"No, I will not wake up. I think that I will stay in the dream," was his answer.

She wiped away her tears and smiled at him. He smiled back and quickly asked, because he knew what floated in her head.

Intuitive.

"Would you?"

"No." Her answer was immediate, deep, and powerful.

She held the rest of the snack out and asked him, as more tears ran down her cheeks, "Want the other half? I will break it in two."

He shook his head, gently took the snack out of her hand, and placed it upon the table. He grasped her hands, and they held onto each other. Lost in the dreams.

It had been a particularly wearisome day.

Word of Mouth

From: Flashes, Sparks, and Shorts: Flash Two

It was the 4th day of March.

"I can't understand this! I have digested every angle of the situation and it makes no sense! We offered a national coupon on them and the sales skyrocketed just a few months ago!" The national sales manager for the Wizard Mills cereal company shouted out to his assistant as he studied the sales chart. His assistant blinked and made some notes on a pad. Actually, she wrote down that she needed to pick up milk from the supermarket on the way home because she really was not interested in the latest lament from her boss. He was generally clueless.

Today was no different.

"Until a month or so ago, Zippy-Os used to be our best-selling cereal that we packaged under thousands of store-brand names in thousands of stores across the nation!"

"I don't know, but the big chief wants to see you at three o'clock in the afternoon tomorrow in the executive conference room to discuss the plummeting sales of Zippy-Os," the assistant said while she fixed her wayward bra strap, wrote "eggs" down on her pad and then added, "our formerly best-selling cereal." The assistant worked a quick smile on her face, and added, "His words. Not mine."

The sales manager swallowed hard.

"I love that you take such copious notes. We need answers for the big chief," the clueless dope said as the assistant nodded her head and wrote down "bread" on the pad.

Clueless.

"No more shipments of Zippy-Os to the northern districts! Hold all those pallets!" The warehouse manager said to his foreman as he moved some pallets of Zippy-O's cereal to a production location in the warehouse.

"What? Why? Last month we could not ship 'em fast enough."

"Dunno. Orders all cancelled," the warehouse manager said with a shrug of his shoulders.

"No more boxes for Zippy-Os!" The print shop manager called out to his crew. Move production over to Fruity Circles!"

"What? Why? Last month we could not print 'em fast enough."

"Dunno. Orders all cancelled," the print shop manager said with a shrug of his shoulders.

"No more shipments of grains and oats for Wizard Mills!" The shipping manager for the farm production called out to his crew.

"What? Why? Last month we could not ship 'em fast enough."

"Dunno. Orders all cancelled," the shipping manager said with a shrug of his shoulders.

"But we have bushels and bushels of 'em backed up forever in the warehouse. They all got that weird-ass preservative chemical sprayed on 'em. What the hell we gonna do wid 'em? Even the cows hate 'em."

"Dunno."

The supermarket store manager shook his head and

scratched the top of the same head as his eyes scanned the multitude of unsold boxes on Zippy-Os on his cereal aisle shelves.

"I don't get it," the store manager mumbled, "just a few weeks ago we couldn't keep them in stock."

He married her late in his life. He was almost fifty-five; she was in and around thirty. She was Latino; he was not. She was beautiful, and he for his age, was very handsome. Nearing retirement and alone for many years, he needed someone to take care of him in his later years. Sure, it raised a few eyebrows and whispers, when they married but they did not care and they were very happy. She kept him well, his house well, he provided well, and they lived a quiet life.

She loved him and he loved her. There were nights of glorious passion, there were laughs and joys and they were happy.

He was an electrician. For twenty-five years. They saved for retirement. Every penny. They wanted to travel. She wanted to show him her homeland, and he wanted to see it.

They lived in an apartment in a walk-up tenement in the middle of Paterson, New Jersey. It was not fancy, but it was clean and bright and fairly safe. The apartment sat within a Latino community and everyone looked out for one another.

The day was the 4th day of February.

"Say, honey, I love this cereal. These store-brand Zippy-O's that I was buying the last few weeks since I had a coupon for them are great. Only a dollar twenty-three for a box too! The same size as that brand name fancy cereal that is over four bucks! Big savings," the handsome husband said to his pretty wife. He poured them in a bowl, settled into his chair, poured the milk on them, took a big shovel-full, and dumped them in his mouth.

"Think retirement, baby!"

"Crunch, crunch, and crunch."

"Wanna spoonful, honey? They are great."

The pretty wife screwed her beautiful mouth up on her pretty face and shook her head to indicate that she did not want any Zippy-Os.

"What? Why?"

The pretty wife took a bite of her whole-wheat toast.

"I tried them last week, and at first, they taste good, but after a few chews they have a weird after-taste. Like preservatives or chemicals, or something."

The handsome husband stared at the cereal, took a spoonful, and deposited it in his mouth.

"Crunch, crunch and crunch."

He swallowed and licked his lips a little. His handsome mouth screwed up like a corkscrew on his handsome face and he nodded.

"Geez. Ya right. They do have a weird after-taste. Yuck. They suck. I never noticed it before now."

"Sorry. Just being honest, honey. I will make you some toast."

The pretty wife spoke to her best friend on the third floor. The women sailed along in Spanish and spoke about meals for their husbands and families. The pretty wife was very social and a chatterbox. The subject of breakfast arrived on her lips.

"Those Zippy-Os are horrible." The pretty wife spoke in Spanish, except for the Zippy-Os part of the conversation . . . where she spoke in English. "They have a weird aftertaste."

The older woman on the fifth floor joined the conversation. She had bought them with a coupon. About a month ago. She nodded her head, as did the woman from the sixth floor. The woman with six children and one more on the way. Money was tight for them. She too, had a coupon.

The maintenance man changing a light bulb in the apartment hallway overheard the conversation, and he listened carefully. He too had bought them with a coupon.

"Ya know," the handsome husband said to his buddy as they sat down on an electrical transformer to eat their lunch, "my wife gave me her honest opinion of those Zippy-Os and they suck. They have a weird aftertaste. I never noticed it until she pointed it out to me."

His partner opened his lunch pail and pulled out his sandwich and said, "I thought ya loved 'em? I went out and bought a box because you told me about them. The wife had a coupon."

"Don't try 'em. Chuck 'em. They suck. I am gonna stop and buy the brand-name on my way home tonight. No more bargain basement cereal for me. Life is too short to eat weird-ass cereal."

His partner nodded and took a bite of the sandwich.

The assistant picked up the items on her shopping list on the way home from work. Out of curiosity, she wandered into the cereal aisle. Her eyes scanned the shelves. There were the Zippy-Os boxes of cereal. Boxes and boxes of them untouched on the shelf. Price reduced to ninety-nine cents. There was also an aisle teaser display full of boxes and boxes of Zippy-O's. Untouched.

She reached for a box when a tall, handsome man cleared his throat and said, "Don't buy 'em. They suck."

She looked up, and he was buying the fancy store brand version of the same cereal.

"They do? Why?"

"Horrible after-taste. Weird. Like preservatives or chemicals, or something. Not worth it."

She nodded and placed the box of Zippy-Os back on the shelf. She checked him out while he walked away and raised her eyebrows. Handsome man. Nice butt and build.

"I want answers! Now!" The big chief of Wizard Mills screamed at his sales team. "Until you clowns ran a coupon promo, Zippy-Os brought the house down. Well?" The big chief's face was red as he scanned his silent sales team, led by the clueless national sales manager. The sales chart projected on the wall behind the big chief told the story. The little red arrow went straight down. Beginning in the second week of February.

The assistant shut the lamp off on the projector and leaned back in her chair. No one had any answers as they shuffled the papers in front of them and studied them. Clueless.

She raised her hand and it surprised everyone when she did so. The big chief nodded at her, thinking she was going to ask if they wanted water, or coffee or tea.

"Yes!" He screamed at the interruption.

"If I might ask. When did we add weird-ass chemicals or change the usual preservatives to Zippy-Os?"

"Huh? What?"

"Preservatives. Chemicals." She crossed her legs and added, "Were they always in there? Because Zippy-Os taste awful. Weird aftertaste. They suck."

An executive on the far end of the conference room table shuffled papers, studied some data, and spoke up quickly,

"We changed the formula in January of this year. Upon a recommendation from R&D for longer shelf life for the big promotional campaign."

The big chief cleared his throat.

She really enjoyed the view from the office of the national sales manager for Wizard Mills. A fancy corner office with a wet bar. Dark oak trim and finishes. She pulled out a note pad and wrote down her shopping list on her new oak desk. The note pad had her name on it and new title too. The desk was underneath the promotional campaign poster for the best-selling cereal for Wizard Mills. "Fruity Circles" now led the way. No weird-ass preservatives.

The new national sales manager needed to pick up a few things on the way home.

Prayers We Used to Pray

From: Flashes, Sparks, and Shorts: Flash Two

The hospice nurse just left. The sound of the door closing echoed some type of finality to the situation. She said that it would not be much longer. The death rattle in her mother's throat had not begun. Its arrival loomed. The daughter clenched her mother's hand. There was nothing else left to do. The daughter administered the pain medication on the specified intervals. Her mother seemed peaceful.

Her mother had not spoken a word or opened her eyes in two days now, so when she stirred as the daughter was nodding off in her chair, the daughter nearly jumped out of her seat. Her mother's eyes opened wide, and she seemed to smile.

"Mommy? I am here," the daughter said as tears filled her eyes. Her mother's eyes wandered, and it seemed as if they finally found her daughter's face. With a slow, agonizing movement, she reached up and ran her gnarled fingers over her dear daughter's face and the words arrived in a low whisper, "Please, pray the prayers that we used to pray. At bedtime, my dear Hannah. Please."

Her mother's eyes snapped shut.

"I will, Mommy. I remember them all. I love you. Now, I lay me down to sleep. . .."

There was no death rattle. Only a peaceful passing of a long and blessed life. The daughter was grateful for that fact.

When her own daughter was old enough to understand, she told her at bedtime, "Here, my dear daughter. Let's read together the prayers that your grandmother and I used to pray. You watch my fingers on the words and I will read them."

"Okay, Mommy."

"Now, I lay me down to sleep. I pray the Lord my soul. . . ."

The hospice nurse just left. The sound of the door closing echoed some type of finality to the situation. She said that it would not be much longer. The death rattle in her mother's throat had not begun. Its arrival loomed. Her daughter clenched her hand, and she reeled in shock when her mother's eyes opened wide and they searched the room. When they found her dear daughter's face; she smiled.

"Please, my dear daughter. Let's go on this journey now. Together. Please pray the prayers we used to pray. Together."

Amidst the flood of tears, her daughter did the best she could as the words of the prayers came out within choked and painful emotions.

"I love you, Mommy. I remember all the prayers. This one was always my favorite. Now, I lay me down to sleep. I pray the Lord my soul. . .."

It was a peaceful passing. The dreaded death rattle did not arrive. Only the prayers.

Healing

From: Flashes, Sparks, and Shorts: Flash Two

It was an American Beech tree; smooth bark, unblemished, tall, and proud, and it was thirty years old. The tree had seen some things but still had a long way to go. Can you only imagine the wondrous stories that you can tell if you stood in one place for one-hundred-years?

She was a dark-eyed beauty, long brown hair that sparkled in the sunlight, a perfect figure, and a perfect smile. The gentle breeze blew a few strands of hair in front of her face and caused her ankle-length dress to float around her ankles. There she stood with the penknife in her one hand and her other hand upon the trunk of the tree.

The young man carefully studied his lover as she asked, "If I carve a heart and our initials and our love into the trunk of this tree, will it make us forever?"

Initially, he did not know how to answer her, and he shifted uncomfortably on his feet.

His voice came out in a stammer, "Ah, ah, I don't know. Maybe. I mean," he pointed at the tree and added, "trees can heal. I mean the scars. They grow new bark and the scars fade away."

He allowed his eyes to wander from her face to the trunk of the tree while he continued to point and he pretended to be an expert in arboriculture.

"It looks as if it is a young tree."

Her eyes rimmed with tears at his answer. She deeply loved him, and that was not the answer that she wanted to hear.

He felt and observed her hurt and cleared his throat and said, "I mean, it is just a carving. A stamp in time. It does not prove our love. Does it? I love you deeply, yet love is complex. Please don't live too far ahead of us. Live and love for every month, every day, every hour and every minute, or better yet, let's live for every second that we are together. Please, let's not miss any of this because it could disappear all too soon. I am afraid that if we look too far ahead in time and in our love, then it will leave us too soon. I always want to be here with you. In this park and on this path with this glorious tree." He took a deep breath and added, "I want to be here, both now and forever, so yes, carve us into the tree and . . . marry me. The tree will forgive us for the pain and it will heal."

She smiled and her tears disappeared.

Each step he took was painful. It was difficult to recall exactly where along the path that the tree was. It had been at least forty years since he walked this path. His memory was vague now of so many things, except for her lingering beauty and their long and endless love.

Glioblastoma.

He did not even know how to say the word properly. She went away so fast. In an instant.

His eyes spotted the tree. He was sure of it; positive, and as much as his old legs could move, he increased his gait while remaining focused on the trunk of the tree. Within what seemed as if it was a few lifetimes, but actually was just a minute or two, he reached the base of the tree. His eyes first scanned the crown and then worked down the trunk. Oh, how the tree had grown! Yet here it was on the trunk! Still there—clear and deep and concise.

He reached out his trembling hand, touched the heart, and lovingly ran his fingers through the carving. Touching, caressing, and capturing the feel and the love.

The tree had not healed and neither will he. The tree bled and so did he. They were kindred souls.

Yet, the tree forgave them for the wound because the tree felt their love.

Now and forever.

A Quiz on Random Francis Albert Sinatra Appearances

From: Flashes, Sparks, and Shorts: Flash Two

"In the middle of July, if Francis Albert Sinatra randomly shows up on your front lawn of your home in Florida at seven o'clock in the morning and croons *In the Wee Small Hours* into a classic #44 chrome microphone, you should:

A: Immediately put the house up for sale and move to Alaska. It is too cold in Alaska, even in July, for Sinatra to croon on your front lawn. Besides, it is too damn hot in Florida, anyway.

B: Bring Francis a generous pour of whiskey in a rocks glass with four ice cubes and a splash of water.

C: Look around and try to find the time machine that Francis used to get to your front lawn (since unfortunately, Sinatra died in 1998) because time machines come in handy to keep in your garage.

D: Stop being so damn cheap and upgrade to a better quality of Scotch whiskey that does not cause hallucinatory behavior.

E: Stop eating spicy food before bedtime.

D: Try to forget about the entire incident, let Francis sing, put a coin box on a folding table in the yard to make a few bucks, turn the air conditioning thermostat down to 66 degrees and go back to bed.

E: Don't worry about it because you are not in Florida but

you are really in Hoboken, New Jersey in 1947. Please see the aforementioned, time machine information.

F: Check for proper local laws, taxes, permits, and licenses required for time machines. Nowadays there is a permit, tax, and license for everything.

G: All of the above."

A Somewhat Correct Answer

G: All of the above

Lucrative Noises

From: Flashes, Sparks, and Shorts: Flash Three

They were best friends. Very dedicated to each other in the daily flow of life, and they shared many things and many laughs. Highs and lows. Daily, they leaned on each other for support and for guidance. They were friends that loved and supported each other through thick and thin. Not all love has to be physical. Often, that is the best love.

He was old and worn out; yet, resilient. Tough as nails. He lived a thousand lives.

She was young, and tested, and resilient, too.

They loved each other in a very special sort of way. He was very conservative, and she was wide open. That was a perfect combination to cover all aspects of life.

Life dealt her some terrible twists and turns and the breakup of her marriage resulted in some extreme pain.

Financial and mental. Pain is pain.

Her ex-husband did not support her emotionally, but he was an excellent provider. Currently, the major trouble was cash flow.

Yet, she was resilient.

Everything was horrible, and she had to move on the spur of the moment. In the mid-summer heat of the old city in a nearby high-rise apartment house, she found an affordable apartment; not the greatest neighborhood and the parking was a wandering adventure, but the apartment was affordable and rather neat and tidy. The best friend and her family moved her and the meager belongings left over from the divorce, and her precious cat, into the new apartment on the spur of the moment.

It was at least 95 degrees and rising, and the humidity was oppressive. Her apartment was on the tenth floor.

The service elevator had a two-hour window of availability. It was all very stressful.

The service elevator moved at a snail's pace. . ..

They all survived.

Barely.

Three weeks after she moved in, she phoned up her best friend.

"The main air conditioning unit in the living area of the apartment is making a terrible noise. It is a very loud rattle, and the noise is scaring the cat. I shut it off, and it is so hot in here."

"Well, you can go into the bedroom and hang out there."

"The cat wants to run all over."

"Did you call maintenance?"

"I did. They cannot come for two days. You are very mechanically inclined and you know everything. Can you come and look at it?"

They loved each other in a very special sort of way.

He was there within an hour. With his tools.

"I am not sure I should touch this unit. We might get in trouble with building maintenance."

"Oh bullshit. They can't come for days. Oh, by the way. I am down to my last nickels. It took all that I had to move in here. Can you loan me a few bucks until next paycheck? I am three hundred dollars short on the rent. Rent is due in four days."

He blinked and said, "Okay. Well . . . I guess, but I am tight now too. You already owe me a grand. We will see."

He bent down, used his tools, and took the cover off the air-conditioning unit and shined his flashlight up into the unit. He poked and prodded and spun the fan blower and the motor and then spoke with surprise.

"Oh my. I see the trouble. Some prior tenant used this unit as a bank."

With a puzzled look on her face, she leaned in to watch as he took a pair of needle-nose pliers and reached into the unit to grab and remove something from the blower motor.

"One hundred. Two Hundred. Three hundred. Four Hundred. Five hundred."

He plucked five one-hundred-dollar bills from the inside of the unit with his pliers and individually dropped them on the floor of the apartment. Then he shined his flashlight back into the until and grabbed some additional items. He dropped two thin dimes on the floor next to the bills.

And twenty cents.

"Five hundred dollars and twenty cents. You just made rent plus one hundred dollars extra."

She smiled. She was in shock. He replaced the cover on the unit as she gathered up the money. No more noises. The apartment was cool within minutes.

"We should go dancing and have dinner and drinks."

"You should save the money."

"Okay, we will only spend the extra one hundred dollars on dinner and drinks."

"You should save the money and put it to next month's rent."

They danced the night away together. In each other's arms. Holding each other's souls tight. Within the whispers, and within the laughter, there was kindness and gentleness and many other good things. Special things that very few people ever share.

They loved each other in a very special sort of way. He was very conservative, and she was wide open. That was a perfect combination to cover all aspects of life.

Lucrative noises.

The Wallet

From: Flashes, Sparks, and Shorts: Flash Three

It was a wispy type of early October day. The kind of day that makes you appreciate the cooler temperatures and the fact that the hiss and anger of summer were in the rear-view mirror.

A gentle wind blew from the north-west; yet it was a purposeful wind. Perhaps the wind in its exceptional glory; really was telling everyone a story.

The leaves on the trees turned upside down in the wind and they displayed some hints of some glorious colors. Just on the edges of the leaves. It was early October and by Halloween, these colors would light up the sky and the world.

She was a wispy type of gal! Gorgeous in style, in presence, and in thoughts.

Very Bohemian in her manner of style, in her choice of dress, and in her general vibe of life. Usually, her long black hair tumbled down her back and licked the outer edges of her waist; except today, where she decided to allow her dear mum to braid it into two glorious braids. Her dress was long, and it was colorful, with blues and yellows, and a very wide patch of red swatches sewn in an inviting "V" shape while surrounding her chest. The dress was wide open at her chest and the dress wisped low upon her body and it had fringe on the ends; ankle high suede boots with wide laces, and a side zipper, and a wide brown hat with weathered edges perched upon her head. Underneath her dress, she wore a tight faded brown shirt, that despite years, was no worse for the wear and that displayed her perky but perfect breasts. No bra. She preferred the free and bouncy lifestyle. A hippie at heart.

In some small circles, they called her the Bohemian Gal. Rightly so. She was thirty years old now and still single, and her mother reminded her of those facts often. In Bohemian Gal's estimation, it was too often. In her many Bohemian ways, she smoked some weed at night and sipped some red wine, too. Harmless activities.

She went shopping every Sunday morning at the same neighborhood food store. Kind of, sort of, bought the same things every trip. Milk, bread, eggs, chicken breasts, a bag of chips, and such.

The Bohemian Gal pushed her shopping cart across the parking lot. Into the gentle wind and the upturned leaves and the untold stories.

The flash of brown and very worn leather caught her eye. The wallet sat right next to the parking space next to her parked car. Her car had peeling paint and bald tires.

There was no car parked there now. Apparently, it was now long gone and the driver's or a passenger's wallet was mistakenly left behind. Remnants of an adventure.

She picked the wallet up and thumbed through it, hoping to identify the rightful owner. It was owned by a mystery man with an unknown name. Ironically, he was born the same year as she was. There were some papers and a few meager dollar bills, and some plastic cards that pushed around debt and postponed the monetary commitment of thirty days under the influence of extreme penalties, and some dust within the folds.

His driver's license was expired.

There was a loyal shopper's card for the food store inside. A thought!

Maybe the store could trace him via that information. She would not venture to the address on the expired driver's license. Too far, and too risky. Bohemian Gal kept a tiny circle.

Bohemian Gal sympathized with the rightful owner. She was honest; and had only a few extra nickels to her name and knew the plight of everyday life. In keeping with her Bohemian ways, she did not own a wallet. She kept her papers in the brown suede bag, slung across her shoulders. It had five individual pockets. Ever quirky, Bohemian Gal held together her important items with a blue rubber band. About a quarter inch thick.

"I found this wallet in the parking lot next to where I parked. I hope you can trace the owner via the loyal shopper's card inside the wallet."

Bohemian Gal explained to the customer service clerk at the service counter. The clerk's eyes went up and down Bohemian Gal.

Her unusual attire and her glorious female figure. He was a young man, and she was stunning, and unusual, and very appealing.

"Thank you. We will reach out to the owner as best as we can. Hopefully, we have the information on file via the loyal shopper's card. I am sure the owner will be very appreciative of your honesty. Do you want to leave your name and contact info in case we find the owner and they want to thank you?"

"No . . . thank you. Please do your best to find him."

It was a fateful late October day. The day that makes you know that November looms on the horizon. Christmas was now a blip on the calendar's radar.

He parked in the same place in the food store's parking lot every time that he shopped there. She was stunning. His eyes went up and down her dress and her body and her long braids.

'Very bohemian in nature,' he thought. He loved the brown hat perched upon her head.

A wind blew from the north. It was a powerful wind, and it blew her dress all around her ankles. The sunlight illuminated her dress. He tried not to look at the silhouette of her bare breasts underneath the folds of her dress, highlighted by the magic of the setting sun.

He failed.

She was parked next to him. And she smiled a smile that could melt an iceberg. Her car had peeling paint and bald tires.

His did, too.

Her eyes went up and down his face, his body, and she loved his floppy hat on his head and the beaded charka stone chain that hung around his neck. A hippie's attire. He was stunning.

"Hi."

"Hi there."

"By chance," he paused and then found the courage to ask, "did you happen to find my wallet here on the ground a few weeks ago? In this very spot."

She smiled a smile that could melt an iceberg and shyly shifted her feet. He smiled in return.

Six months later, the Bohemian Gal and the Bohemian Guy, married.

It was a joyous occasion. For wedding gifts, they gave each other matching wallets.

She was a wispy gal, and he was a purposeful man.

On their wedding day, the April wind blew out of the south.

It was a gentle but a purposeful wind. Perhaps the wind in its extraordinary glory; really was telling everyone their story.

A Few Beers with Jesus

From: Flashes, Sparks, and Shorts: Flash Three

Every Tuesday for about five years, they met for beers at the local gin joint. Fifth and Main Street. It was a family joint. Nothing fancy, but the beer was always cold. Pints were still only four bucks. They met here many years ago; became drinking buds. The two Jersey guys just hit it off and now they had a tradition. Except if Tuesday fell on a holiday.

Matt and Dave.

Matt was seventy-nine years young. Long since retired from a job as a car salesman. He made a good living. Solid enough to be fairly comfortable in his retirement. His wife was two years younger than he was and she was getting along well enough, too. Their children long since moved away from New Jersey to more affordable states and good jobs. New Jersey, within its glory, had its issues. One child in North Carolina and one in Florida. Three grandchildren.

Dave was eighty-two years old. His wife passed about three years earlier. Cancer. Thankfully, she did not suffer too long. One child in California, but Dave had five grandchildren.

Be fruitful and multiply.

Dave did not see them often, but he spoke on the phone with his family every Saturday afternoon at two.

"So . . . Dave," Matt asked as they nursed their third pint of cold beer, "if you didn't have me to hang out with, have a few beers with . . . who would you have a few with?"

Dave answered right away.

"Jesus. I would like to have a few beers with Jesus."

Matt almost spit his beer out, but instead, he swallowed hard and moved on.

"Jesus? Really? Why?"

"I need to ask Him a few questions. I think He would be a cool guy to hang out with, too," Dave said as he drained his last drop and waved to Old Phil, the bartender, for a refill. Dave pointed at Matt's beer, too. Then he pointed at his chest to signal the tab designation. Phil dropped them.

"Doesn't Jesus prefer wine?" Matt asked as he sipped the last drop of his pint and dug into the fresh one.

"Nope. Wine is reserved for a much more sacred occasion."

"Fair enough. What would you ask Him, Dave?"

"Lots. First off . . . was Lazurus a good friend? Like you and I are? Drinking buddies?"

"His answer?"

"Yup. I cried because he was. Friends are forever and Jesus was human, just like us. He knows our pain at the loss of loved ones."

Dave took a long sip of beer and it was apparent that the beer was softening him up.

"Gotcha. Next on the question list?"

"Geez. God sent so many servants. Moses, Elijah, John, Luke, Abraham, King David, Noah, Peter, John the Baptist, Paul, Daniel, The Archangels, etc. Why did the people still not listen?"

"Good question. What would His answer be?"

Dave pondered it for a moment as Old Phil and some other patrons now listened in.

"Because we are stupid and stubborn and hopeless without Jesus and his willingness to die for us."

Now a crowd gathered.

"Wow! Hard hitting, my old friend. We are stupid?"

"Yup. We sure are. Then I would ask Him if Saint Michael can really kick Satan's backside. Twice. And Jesus would smile, drain His glass of beer, order another one, and politely say, 'No one can beat Saint Michael. It would be no contest.' I would ask Him if that spear in the side hurt and the forty days of fasting really were no fun at all and carrying that cross was super painful and was dying really all that bad. And Jesus would nod His head with tears in His eyes and He would recall all those horrors and quietly say, 'Yes.' But I would ask Jesus, in between all that horror and pain and suffering . . . did he have fun in his time on Earth? How cool was the wedding where you turned the water into wine?"

Old Phil jumped in and entered his opinion.

"I would go for that! Profitable!"

Matt smiled and then turned to Dave and asked, "And His answer would be?"

"Sure, He had fun. Lots of parties. Learned a trade. Made things with His hands. Made friends. Lived a simple life. Never owned a home or had credit cards or debt. Never traveled very far from his home. Slept on dirt floors. Never had a designated parking space, or a fancy office, or a car. Knew pain. Knew joy. Glorified God. He would tell me that the purpose of life is to glorify God. Jesus did that better than anyone else! He healed people. I bet the blind man at the Pool in Bethesda sure celebrated that day!"

Matt took another long sip of beer and nodded his head

in agreement, and spoke in a voice just above a whisper.

"Blind from birth. I can't even imagine the joy."

Silence ensued and set in.

Pensive pondering. Dave had hit a nerve with many of the listeners and fellow patrons.

Old Phil paused in slinging the drinks.

Dave spoke up to break the silence.

"Yup. I would ask Jesus after His third beer—will I see my wife again in Heaven? I loved her so. Jesus would tell me, 'Yes.' Then I would ask, 'Why are we so dumb?' And Jesus would say, 'Because you are, and I once was human.' Then I would ask Him, 'Why did you do it? Why did you die so horribly so that we could live in eternity? When we are so disrespectful, and so arrogant, and so uncaring, and so unrepentant?'"

No one answered.

No one breathed.

Tears rolled down Dave's cheeks as he answered his own fictitious scenario question.

"Jesus would say, 'Because God loves us and that was the mission that God gave to Him to do. To save us. To laugh at Satan and his temptations. There was no other way.' And Jesus would add, 'The best thing that we can ever do for each other is love without judgement. Just love each other. No matter what.'"

Dave drained the last drop of his beer and plopped the empty pint glass on the bar counter.

"Then I would thank Jesus, shake His hand, pay our tabs and be on my way." Dave slid out of his barstool and he wobbled a bit.

"Anyway, this has been profound. Thanks for another

Tuesday, Matt. Today is on me. See you next week. God willing."

Old Phil the bartender hustled over as Dave reached for his wallet. The old bartender shook his head and violently waved his hands in the air.

Phil shouted, "No!" He then lowered his voice to a solemn tone. "This is where the bartender would step in and say, 'No charge. The beers are on the house. Thank you, Jesus, but there is no charge. You already paid your tab in full.'"

Old Phil could not hold back the tears as he struggled to say, "And then some."

Feet in the Lake

From: Flashes, Sparks, and Shorts: Flash Three

She was the love of his life.

He was hers, too.

Forever.

Brown hair that danced along her face and down her back like a zinnia flower bloom, still waving its beauty in the late August wind.

Green eyes as if they were perfect green glass.

Her eyes glowed in the sunlight. In the sunset. In the night.

Glorious beauty. Perfect figure. Perfect facial features, perfect smile, perfect in every way. He was a lucky man.

Late August on the big lake in New Hampshire was a special time of the year. It was a special place. A special time in their lives. Embarking on a new adventure.

The stretch of the lake with the little inlet bay behind the ice cream shoppe was a favorite spot of theirs. This was where they shared ice cream and love and beauty.

One late Saturday night when they were first married, when no one was around; they went skinny-dipping here and then made love in a hidden spot behind the tree line. On a blanket that she brought along. It was her idea and her covert plan to loosen him up. When you are young and in love; life is so easy.

When life was simple and gentle. There were no cellphones available.

He was conservative; she had a hidden wild side. A perfect match.

Today, around 9 PM, as the sun was fading, they stopped and bought some ice cream cones. She loved chocolate, and he loved whatever she loved.

The last sales of the day. The ice cream shoppe closed.

"Let's put our feet in the lake!"

She kicked off her sandals, rolled up the legs of her jeans, and scrambled to their favorite rock. She put her feet in the lake and then waved to her husband for him to join her. He kicked off his boots and rolled up his pants legs and did so.

They enjoyed watching the remaining few boats on the lake cruising to ports in the August sunset, and the beauty, and their love. They shared ice cream kisses. When you are middle-aged and in love; life was a little more difficult but still enjoyable.

"After all these years, do you have any regrets in marrying me?"

"Only one."

Her eyes opened wide in surprise that he had a regret.

"Oh, my. Really? One? Okay. What is it?"

"That you enjoyed vanilla ice cream instead of chocolate."

He did not expect it. Blind-sided. She pushed him into the lake. She laughed, stood up and stripped off her clothes and jumped in after him.

"Emily! Someone will see us!"

She laughed and said, "Who? No one is around! And

who cares? After all, it is just skin that surrounds our soul!"

They made love in a hidden spot behind the tree line. On a blanket that she brought along.

Cellphones were a thing now. They did not use them. No need.

The ice cream shoppe was long since gone. Only the asphalt parking lot and a broken foundation of the shoppe remained. Weeds poked up through the cracks in the asphalt. Overlooking trees wept at the scene. It was very sad. Time had not been kind.

The big lake still was gorgeous and so was his wife.

Hampered by the passage of time and with some very painful and careful steps, he hobbled over to the rock ledge.

She smiled at him and patted the craggily surface for him to sit next to her. He placed his cane aside and, with some considerable trouble and effort, he did so.

"Let's put our feet in the lake!"

She said as she kicked off her shoes and pulled off her socks and rolled up her pants legs. She helped her husband with his.

The lake water was chilly for late August. Colder than she recalled; or was it their circulation?

They enjoyed watching the remaining few boats on the lake cruising to ports in the August sunset, and the beauty, and their love. They shared old age kisses. When you are very old and in love; life is painful but gracious in its last quarter.

"I would ask you about any regrets, but I am afraid of what will happen," the wife said. "The water is cold."

He laughed and said, "Well, yes, it is, and making love on that bank over there might cause some aches and pains."

His wife leaned in and stared into his eyes and his glorious wrinkles that time provided. With all her heart and soul, she loved this wonderful man.

With a wink and a smile, she said, "It might just be worth it. I brought along a blanket."

They made love in a hidden spot behind the tree line. On a blanket that she brought along.

He was conservative; she had a hidden wild side. A perfect match.

She was the love of his life.

He was hers, too.

Feet in the lake.

Forever.

The Tall Grey-Haired Man at the Bus Stop

From: Flashes, Sparks, and Shorts: Flash Three

He was born in April of 1934. Smart as a whip, country boy, tall and handsome and of Scottish descent. Grew up dirt-poor in Amherst County, Virginia; no running water, but they had electricity. Count those blessings.

Haul the grain back and forth from the granary. Grind the grain. Pennies on the dollar, but they all count. Simple life. Great faith.

Persevere.

No tractors; only horses. Work the farm. Survive. Praise God for everything that you received. Fall on your knees. Understand what God gives to you. Every day. Blessings. Cornbread dipped in milk with a side of beans. Mana from Heaven.

The Great Depression meant nothing to them because to actually be poor . . . the implications were that you had to have had money. When you are poor, then you are poor. Can't get nothing from nothing. The old blood from a stone sort of thing.

Even dirt has some friends. They might not be lucrative, but they are friends.

He grew up God-fearing and Jesus-loving. The Holy Spirit was there in the mix, too. He went to church every Sunday and every Wednesday night. Dinner and Bible study.

Tradition and commitment. Hard work was his motivation. No slackers. No laziness ever tolerated. Studied everything and spoke only when he was required to do so.

Purposeful. Words laced with the wisdom of hard times and of wisdom earned.

Sunday night. Singing along to the signals from the radio stations out of Roanoke on an old tube radio. Blowing the grand old Gospel tunes on a harmonica; self-taught on the six-string. Great voice. Music was a backbone of his love; Heaven sent; on the harps of the angels. Music binds us all.

Loving Jesus. Honoring God.

Studying the old scriptures.

Some new ones too.

Met a beauty from nearby Nelson Couty. Courted. Fell in love and married. Moved to the big city of Richmond. Nailed a job with the government. He slowly became a tall, grey-haired man. Full of wisdom and full of love.

Every day, for 47 years, the tall gray-haired man—waited in his suit and tie at the bus stop to the ride the bus to his job, downtown.

Rain, snow, cold, heat, wind, rain . . ..

Appropriate weather gear—so noted.

His loving family would wait for his arrival from the bus stop to their home every day.

Clockwork.

No excuses. There is a reason that they call it work.

The young man was born in Henrico County, Virginia, in 1978.

He grew up within the care of a loving family and

eventually went to school, and every day, his school bus rolled by the city bus stop. Every day his eyes would catch the tall, grey-haired man waiting for the bus.

Every day, the tall gray-haired man waited at the bus stop to the take the bus to his job, downtown.

Rain, snow, heat, wind, rain . . ..

The young man would take note. Grammar school. Then high school. Another summer off. Another fall begins.

Still, the tall grey-haired man stood tall. At the bus stop. Rain, snow, cold, heat, wind, rain . . ..

Finally, college loomed. The young man would leave soon. His life would change. He just had to stop and ask. On the last possible day, he did so. The young man would have to walk to school and be late for the opening bell.

It was worth it.

A long explanation. One simple question.

The tall, grey-haired man smiled and said, "Because it is what I need to do to take care of my family and to glorify God. Our purpose here in this life is very simple; it is to glorify God. There are no excuses. There is a reason that they call it work. In my world, there are no slackers. No laziness ever tolerated."

The young man took in the words of wisdom and went on and did great things in his life.

The tall, grey-haired man contributed to the young man's success. And many others' success, too.

Sadly, after some long health struggles, bolstered by The Lord, the tall grey-haired man passed away at the age of 89 years old.

Married; 68 years. 3 children; 12 grandchildren and 22 great-grandchildren

Legacy.

The tall, grey-haired man at the bus stop touched so many people in his life.

Countless.

The memorial service for the tall, grey-haired man packed the church to the rafters. Many family members and friends shared glorious memories of his life. They all sang the old and the new songs, shared love, and remembered.

It was worth it.

If you never met the tall grey-haired man at the bus stop in this world; then believe in the Lord your God with all your heart and soul, and you will surely meet him someday afterwards.

All assurances. Guaranteed.

It will be worth it.

An Entire Cornball Christmas Romance Story in Ten Sentences

From: Flashes, Sparks, and Shorts: Flash Three

Here we go:

In early November, a super handsome man with fantastic hair and perfect white teeth joins a new company and his beautiful new coworker with fantastic hair and perfect white teeth does not like him.

All the other women in the office fall all over him.

Over a Thanksgiving business lunch, the two handsome and beautiful coworkers bond over some new business deal and then celebrate their success.

Suddenly, they like each other and are no longer enemies.

By the first week in December, they are madly in love.

The second week of December, an evil and jealous woman (Ms. Evil) who does not have fantastic hair and perfect white teeth and works in the same office, spreads a false rumor about Mr. Handsome and something he supposedly is going to do to sabotage Ms. Beautiful's business success while he takes all the credit for the new deal.

Mr. Handsome and Ms. Beautiful argue and break their romance off; even after Mr. Handsome denies it.

On Christmas Eve in the office, Ms. Evil confesses to her lie after having the Christmas spirit overtake her soul.

Mr. Handsome and Ms. Beautiful make up on Christmas Eve after she breathlessly chases him down a snowy city street when he left the office and was heading to the jewelry store to return the engagement ring that he bought for her.

After Ms. Beautiful says, "I am so sorry" two-hundred and seventeen times, they kiss and make up with fake snow that looks like mothball chips raining down on them and he proposes to her, she accepts, and he gives her the ring.

There you go!

Frozen in Words

From: Flashes, Sparks, and Shorts: Flash Three

"Oh, for the love of Pete! Not again! I can't stand when he does this. Now, who knows when he will get back to us?" The mean, grumpy boss character, Mr. Curley exclaimed as he threw his arms in the air in frustration. "Just when I was going to berate you, Ms. Lawson, for something that you had nothing to do with and was not even your job to begin with!"

The character of Ms. Lawson looked up from her desk in the office setting that the author just described in minutia detail and said, "Well, I, for one, am thrilled that he took a break right now. The last thing that I needed was another unfair berating episode from you, Mr. Curley! This is the fourth chapter in a row that you have berated me! And I am rather tired of it."

The character known as Mr. Curley pulled out a chair from the desk next to where Ms. Lawson sat, and he sat down in it.

He waved his hands in the air and said, "Well, don't blame me. Blame him! I did not ask to be the mean, grumpy boss in this book. He made me do it!"

The character known as Lemmy, who is the porter and maintenance person in the office setting, was emptying trashcans when the pause occurred. He held the trashcan in his hand and looked at the other fellow characters.

Lemmy said, "I ain't very happy, either. This clown of a

writer made me have a terrible drinking habit. I am on the edge of being fired, and now, because he took another break, I am stuck holding this trashcan in my hand for who knows how long now? How long do you think he is going to be gone this time? Last time, I stood for two days in one spot while tossing trash in the smelly trash compactor on the loading dock!"

The character of the office receptionist, Matilda, called out from her reception desk in the lobby of the office. "Who knows? As usual, he is drinking beer while he writes so he might be off for a bathroom break or he might be half-in-the-bag. Ha! He made you a drunk. Must have modeled you after himself. Don't feel bad. I have crooked teeth and a bad hairstyle and my husband is unemployed and I have to support the entire house on my own."

"Hey! Back to our spots! He is back," Mr. Curley called out. "Oh, wow! Hold on tight! He is pulling us out of the office!"

Ms. Lawson and the character of Mr. Curley sat together in a fancy restaurant setting just described by the author when the writing stopped. The two characters sat at their table and waited for the typing to resume.

"I can't believe that after six hours of typing now we are in a restaurant on Christmas Eve and sharing a romantic dinner and drinking wine, Mr. Curley. I mean, three chapters ago you were berating me."

"Yeah, Ms. Lawson, that is how these corny Christmas romance stories go. One minute we are at each other's throats and can't stand each other, and the next minute we are madly in love. Say this wine is rather good. I think it is going to my head. I think we are going to kiss soon. I mean, will you mind that? I never noticed how beautiful you are and how green your eyes are, Ms. Lawson."

The character of Ms. Lawson smiled rather bashfully

and toyed with her wineglass.

"Oh, thank you, Mr. Curley. That is very nice of you. No . . . I don't think I will mind at all. Say, what is your first name? I don't think he has mentioned it yet. Must be a mistake on his part that his editor will catch. You are very handsome."

"Alex. Yours?"

"Annabelle."

"Lovely name. Do you think we will get married and have children?"

"Most likely. I sure hope he returns soon. I so want another sip of wine and that kiss," Ms. Lawson said as she blushed with the words.

Mr. Curley smiled just as the typing began once more.

"Do you, Alex, take Annabelle as your lawfully wedded wife, to love now and forever more?" the character of the preacher asked, as the snow fell outside the church.

"I do," the character of Alex answered.

"Do you, Annabelle, take Alex as your lawfully wedded husband, to love now and forever more?"

"I do," the character of Annabelle answered.

"You may kiss the bride," the preacher character said, and, they did so.

As they walked hand-in-hand up the center aisle of the church, as the characters of the celebrating attendees of the ceremony cheered and clapped, the character of Alex leaned in and asked the character of his new wife, "I am sure glad he took those breaks and the writer froze us in the words. He needed those breaks to write such an amazing story. It sure turned out wonderfully. I love you, Annabelle."

The character of Annabelle said, "I agree. And I love you, too, Alex. I sure hope Lemmy and Matilda are happy now, too."

"Oh, they are. We all are just characters in this cornball, Christmas romance book. That is how they all go. It is not reality but it sure is fun to escape with. Everyone ends up happy. Now and forever more."

The Toy Soldier

From: Flashes, Sparks, and Shorts: Flash Three

The little boy wished as hard as he could for a toy soldier for Christmas.

A soldier named Joe.

He had faith in Santa Claus.

His parents had very little in the way of extra spending money; yet, they pinched their pennies to make their children's dreams at Christmastime come true. As best as they could.

Let's be clear here; no one was receiving a diamond necklace for Christmas.

Or a new car.

The little boy had an older sister. She had her own dreams.

The toy soldier named Joe slept under the glory of the family's Christmas tree in a box with gaily decorated elves and reindeer and topped by a red bow.

Until the joy of Christmas morning revealed his power.

The little boy jumped for joy when he saw Joe for the first time.

His sister received her coveted curling iron as a gift. To curl her gorgeous black locks of hair. Her package had a red bow, too.

The little boy danced in joy, along with Joe, all around

the Christmas tree.

Joe was a tough guy. He had a deep red scar on his face—fully equipped with painted, yet authentic, oozing blood.

Joe took his lumps in combat. Now Joe had combat wounds. Serious wounds from battles. As many of us have, too.

Joe did not smile or laugh; he was a toy soldier. Equipped for a backyard-make-believe battle. His box had cool "Joe" logos and fantastic illustrations of Joe attacking the enemy for the better good of humankind.

Joe had fantastic accessories in his box to assist him and the little boy in their make-believe battles. In the backyard of his imagination.

Joe had dog tags, he had a plastic rifle, and a knife, and a backpack, and slip-on plastic boots. He wore authentic battle fatigues with button snaps, and a pot on his head, with a chin strap, and his naked plastic body had incredible muscles.

Joe never died in battle or in any other walk of life.

On endless missions, Joe saved his sister's best friend named Barbie and her less-than-rugged boyfriend named Ken, from persons with nefarious intentions. Joe was undefeatable. A hero.

Together, the little boy and Joe saved the world.

Joe slept on a barrack rack, with a tissue for a blanket. He had a footlocker with extra boots and knives and a dress uniform for parades.

One day, Joe went into the swimming pool and he saved Barbie again. The next morning after that mission, the little boy found Joe severely wounded. His internal metal hooks had rusted and his head and arm popped off! His rubber bands that made him flexible broke. Oh no!

Tears!

But there are other heroes in this world. The little boy's father patiently repaired Joe in a long surgical procedure. On the workbench in the basement. New hooks and rubber bands. Joe's head tilted to the side a little. The little boy did not mind. Battle scars. We all have them.

Joe never died in battle or in any other walk of life.

The little boy grew into a teenager and then he grew into a young man. Joe's missions dried up, and he retired to a dusty old box. Along with his fantastic accessories and his foot locker. Joe always wore his dog tags. So that everyone knew he was Joe.

Along came a girlfriend and then a beautiful wife, and a marriage and a job. Then two beautiful little children and a little puppy named Jingles.

Joe went along for the ride. In his dusty old box. Sadly, there were still no missions; therefore, Joe, like a good toy soldier, waited, and he waited and he waited.

Years rolled on and the dust grew deeper.

Joe waited for his mission while staying in his dusty old box, along with hockey ice skates, a hockey goalie mask, a set of hockey goalie gloves, an old beanbag toy frog, a few baseball cards, a toy robot, and an old baseball. Forgotten in the walk of life.

Then the fateful day arrived. It was a Saturday.

A little boy crept into the attic of their home along with Jingles and together they explored the dust and the past and went in search of hidden treasures. Summer vacation from school was always the time to go in search of hidden treasures. August was here and September was, in a little boy's mind, still ages away.

"Wow! The little boy exclaimed as he found the dusty old box and opened it up. Out of all the treasures that he found, it was Joe that caught his eyes and invoked adventures as Jingles lifted his paws up on the side of the box to peer inside. The little boy gathered Joe up in his hands, along with his fantastic accessories, and his foot locker.

Along with Jingles, they rushed downstairs to find his father in the living room reading a book.

"What is this cool toy, Dad?"

The father lifted his eyes and smiled and said, "Why, that is Joe. He is my old toy soldier. I forgot about Joe. You must have found him in that old dusty box. Santa brought him one year for Christmas, and we were great friends and together, we beat all the bad guys and we saved the world."

The father motioned to his son for him to hand Joe off and the father held Joe in his hands and Joe's tilted head reminded him of the battle scars, of other heroes now long gone, and of the joy that Joe brought to his life.

He still wore his dog tags.

Joe was ready for a new set of missions. Joe did not smile or laugh, but in his own plastic toy soldier way, Joe smiled at his old friend. The father's mind whirled with the joy of the memories. He handed Joe back off to his son.

"Wow! Joe is so cool! Can we play with him?" The little boy was so happy and enthusiastic.

"Sure," the father said, as he wiped away some tears from his eyes and set his book aside. "Let me tell you all about Joe and we can find him some missions and bad guys to defeat."

"Can we save the world again, Dad?"

"Absolutely, Joe, and Jingles, and you, and me . . . we can do it! Together."

"Why is Joe's head tilted, and it does not bend like his legs and arms do?"

The father smiled and remembered the hero.

"Well, one day Joe went on a mission in our old swimming pool and he broke. I was very sad, but your grandfather, well, he fixed Joe. He operated on him and Joe was wounded, but he was back and better than ever. . .."

Today was Joe's special day but someday, the little boy will revisit the box and bring back to the world and to his walk of life, the hockey ice skates, the hockey goalie mask, the set of hockey goalie gloves, the old beanbag toy frog, the baseball cards, the toy robot, and the old baseball.

Unforgotten in the walk of life.

Joe still wore his dog tags.

Joe never died in battle or in any other walk of life.

He never will.

The Red Barn in the Snow

From: Flashes, Sparks, and Shorts: Flash Three

The quality of the construction of the red barn stood the test of time. Dutch carpenters knew their trade. Old-school skills, sharpened by generations, teaching and tools and quality. Wooden measuring sticks, old-time hand tools, and wooden mallets and pegs.

No stainless steel or cordless drills here. No imperfect or flimsy construction allowed. Craftmanship from a lost era.

The planks of maple were still sturdy and ran perfectly vertical when they had to do so and horizontal when they needed to do so. And the painted white trim and the moldings! Perfect. And the doors had sturdy hinges of black iron and only needed oil after the worst of the winter weather passed through in January and February.

By March the hinges grew creaky.

Outwardly, the red barn was nothing very special. Inwardly, and to the town, it was very special. The red barn sat at the end of a long gravel driveway along the main drag of Midland Avenue, and it harkened to a by-gone era, when chickens explored the plot of land owned by the Van Beusichem family, and some cows wandered around and perhaps, some goats and other livestock. Before Midland Park, New Jersey became a semi-urban little nook in Bergen County, New Jersey.

Every Christmas season, right after Thanksgiving, the old farmer, Mr. Jacob Van Beusichem, climbed up a wooden ladder perched on the front of the red barn and hung the freshest and most glorious Christmas evergreen wreath that the townsfolk, or, for that matter, any other person, ever saw above the double doors to the red barn. It was handmade by Jacob himself, for he, was a very talented craftsman. He picked out the evergreen branches for constructing the wreath himself from nearby wooded areas, adorned with the conifers native to the local, and carefully fit them all together with great care on a wooden and wire frame.

In later years, when electricity arrived at the barn, Jacob framed the entire front of the red barn right to the peak, with blue Christmas lights and a spotlight on the glorious wreath.

Simple joy at Christmastime.

When it snowed, the red barn in the snow was a majestic testimony to the beauty of the Christmas season.

It was a focal point for the town; and every Christmas season, the red barn turned into a historic and beautiful landmark.

Old Jacob Van Beusichem was a carpenter, a dairy and livestock farmer, a metal worker, and many other things. He also was a perfectionist; from an era when workers took pride in what they did. Craftsmen. The farmhouse that his family built a few hundred yards from the red barn was also a work of art. The wrap-around farmer's porch was magnificent. The old big green Dutch Christian Reformed church on Midland Avenue had many generations of Dutch families and the Van Beusichem family remained faithful parishioners.

When old Jacob passed away, the family sold off parcels of the land of the sprawling farm, as Midland Park changed, but the red barn stood tall.

And every year, the family decorated the red barn with the same lights and a majestic evergreen Christmas wreath.

Old Jacob had taught his sons his secrets.

The red barn was a wonderful holiday memory for a very young boy. The young boy loved the Christmas season, and it fascinated him and overcame the little boy with joy when the season rolled around. Right after Halloween, the anticipation grew. Oh! To see Christmas through a child's eye! It is truly a special time. October, November, and then blessed December. The heat of summer is a distant memory and the gloom of mid-to-late-January is, but a distant, yet slightly ominous, thought.

It was best not to linger there; instead, it is always best to focus on the current joy that Christmas and December bring to our lives.

Every Christmas, the little boy would anxiously await the arrival of the majestic wreath above the doors to the red barn. On the first night, right after Thanksgiving, after sunset, the little boy would run the few blocks from his home on a side street off Midland Avenue to where the red barn sat at the end of that long gravel driveway. Now, new buildings stood here and there and everywhere, but the parcel where the farmhouse stood and the red barn stood remained. The chickens and the cows, and the livestock were gone; but the glory of the red barn remained.

Every year, he would jump for joy at the sight of it. It was a highlight of the season for him and many others. It stuck in the little boy's mind forever.

He was very old now. His back ached and his eyesight was poor, and he leaned north and south at the same time. His steps were painful, but the memories remained. Right after Thanksgiving, he begged his son to take him there. To the base of the gravel driveway along Midland Avenue in Midland Park, New Jersey. He just had to know if the red barn was still there. And the wreath and the spotlight and the blue lights that ran to the peak.

One last time.

His son agreed.

On the day that his son picked him up from the nursing home to drive him the forty minutes or thereabouts to Midland Park, it snowed. All the better. They parked along Midland Avenue and the old man looked all around at everything that had changed since he last visited. Many things. Of course, time and change always arrive.

The big green church was now white.

The old man stood with his son at the base of the gravel driveway as the tears ran down his cheeks. His son wrapped his arm around his father and held him tight. The son also cried at seeing his father's joy over such a simple scene.

Simple, yet it could have adorned a picture-perfect-Christmas-postcard. It was magnificent.

A majestic wreath, highlighted by a spotlight, carefully dug out of the fresh snow so as not to interfere with its beacon. Blue lights framing the front of the barn, right to the peak.

Just as the old man remembered from when he was a little boy. Simple joy at Christmastime. The red barn in the snow was a majestic testimony to the beauty of the Christmas season that stood the test of time.

May we always remember the simple joys of our lives.

Now and forever.

The Ninety-Year-Old Man at the Train Station

From: Flashes, Sparks, and Shorts: Flash Four

The 30th Street west train station is within the confines of the old city. A place amidst layers of travel. A place of legends. A place of hustle and of bustle and where souls crisscross on their way through life. Countless stories, countless lives, and many untold stories of life on the road.

The elderly man had a very thick chock of white hair on his head. His body bent over as he made his way to the wooden bench at the train station. He seemed to be moving with a purpose and with haste in mind. Perhaps he felt that he would be late for his train.

Behind him, he pulled a two-tier set of very chic and modern luggage. A roller-type of case, with a smaller case set on top of the roller bag. Despite it being early June and quite warm outside of the train station in the downtown section of the old city, the man wore a heavy pull-over type of sweater with creased trousers, and dress shoes. He dressed conservatively and old-fashioned, but very smarty and very neatly.

The middle-aged man, while seated on the wooden bench opposite of where the man with the thick white hair hustled over to, studied the elderly man. The middle-aged man wrapped himself up in his own emotions. He was heading home to his family to attend a funeral. That is always a generally horrible situation.

Needless to say, this was not a pleasant trip for the middle-aged man. The deceased loved one was not a blood relative; however, he was a friend as well as a relative. The two of them were very close; so many memories; so many miles together. This old city brought back other memories. A military mission. Uniforms, salutes, persons that he met along the way. Oh, my! How the mind can wander and be wide open at times such as these.

Yet, he remained a keen observer of life all around him. Communion with God and all the saints in Heaven is sacred; yet, sometimes, we need communion with ourselves.

The middle-aged man carefully watched as the elderly gentleman settled onto the wooden bench; he carefully tucked the stack of luggage close to him next to the wooden bench, then looked around, unzipped the zipper on the top set of luggage and reached inside the case. The elderly man pulled out a pair of eyeglasses, then he set them on the bench directly beside to where he was sitting.

The middle-aged man watched as a young woman came by, tugging her luggage behind her. She sat next to the elderly man; just a few feet separated them with the eyeglasses sitting between them on the bench.

The elderly man waited a few seconds for the young woman to settle in, then, he picked up the eyeglasses held them in the air and asked, "Are these your eyeglasses?"

"No," the young woman said, and then she added, "I just sat here. They were there already."

"Oh, okay. I will just leave them here for someone to claim."

The young woman stared at the elderly man for a few seconds, then she seemed uncomfortable. She stood up, grabbed her luggage and off she went into the hustle and the bustle of the train station.

The middle-aged man watched and listened. He realized

the eyeglasses were just a plant for the elderly man to make conversation.

'Loneliness is horrible,' he thought. The elderly man stared across the row and he studied the middle-aged man. Finally, he spoke as he pointed at the middle-aged man's hands.

"You are not married. I see that you do not wear a wedding ring."

"No. Not married."

The elderly man nodded and said, "I am married for sixty years. I am ninety now. My wife is dying of cancer. She is in the hospital. I love her so. I am traveling to see her. It is an awful situation. I try to believe in God, but I cannot. God is taking my wife from me."

"Oh, my. I am very sorry. I wish you and your wife the best and safe travels while you journey to see her. There is always hope that she will recover."

"Yes. Safe travels. No God. No hope. It is sad."

Now, the middle-aged man was uncomfortable. Too many emotions. He stood up, waved in the direction of the elderly man, and tugged on his luggage. He went around the corner by the train announcement board and stood near a wall to wait for his connecting train.

As he stood there, he could hear the elderly man ask, "Are these your eyeglasses?"

A train station police officer wandered by and stood next to the middle-aged man. The officer must have been watching from afar.

"He is harmless. Just lonely. The same thing every day. He lives in an old-folk's home down the street. He comes here to pass the time. Makes believe he is catching a train. Always the same dialogue. Are these your eyeglasses?

Then he moves to the fact that his wife is dying and no belief in God. Apparently, his wife died many years ago. He stays for a few hours, makes conversation, and then leaves."

The middle-aged man nodded.

He thanked the officer for the information and said, "Loneliness is horrible."

"Sure is."

The middle-edged man was now on his flip-flop; on the return trip, and once more, he found himself waiting for the connecting train. It was time to go home.

His emotions were high. It was so difficult to say goodbye. So many tears; so many loved ones reunited.

Funerals and weddings have so many similarities.

As the middle-aged man wandered and waited; remarkably, he spotted the elderly man once again. Seated in the same place. Same wooden bench.

"Are these your eyeglasses?"

He could hear his words.

It was the same time of day as when they first met. Inside his heart, the middle-aged man felt as if he failed the elderly man during that first meeting. The loss of his loved one had some lessons and some caring and some deep feelings associated with the tragic event.

'What was that Bible verse that the priest used during the funeral mass?'

The middle-aged man recalled it, and in haste, he tugged at his luggage and walked over to the elderly man. He reached out for his hands and the elderly man held onto to both.

His old eyes looked up as the middle-aged man said, "I

am sorry about your wife being ill."

"Oh, thank you. I love her so."

"And there is a God."

The elderly man frowned, shook his head, and said, "No. Sorry. I cannot believe in God."

"But you just said you did."

"Sorry? No, I didn't," the elderly man replied.

"Yes, you did. You just said that you love your wife. The Holy Bible tells us that 'He that loveth not knoweth not God; for God is love.' *(KJV) You love. Therefore, you believe in and know God."

The middle-aged man smiled, let go of the elderly man's hands and walked away.

The elderly man smiled and whispered, "Yes. Bless you. Finally, my answer came. There is a God. Because God is love."

Time passes.

Two police officers stood and talked. Under the train announcement board.

"Say, Bill, you seen the old guy from the home lately?"

"Nah. Not in forever. Maybe he died."

"Maybe. I wonder if he ever believed in God?"

"Dunno."

He did.

* (1 John 4:8.) The Holy Bible, King James Version. Cambridge Edition: 1769.

A Line of Stones

From: Flashes, Sparks, and Shorts: Flash Four

There was a time long ago when the borough on the outskirts of the old city was innocent.

Now, you had to search to find innocence. Search very, very hard. It was there, just shrouded by wear and tear, and haggardness.

Marcus was a curious and innocent sort of little boy. Now that he was eleven years old, he could hold his own. Already street-smart and wise and intelligent to the ways of life and the intricacies and nooks of an old city.

Both the evils and the good.

Marcus lived in a humdrum house, on a busy street, in a borough of the city; his house was within a few steps of a bus stop on the main bus line. The bus ran up and down the main street most of the day and well into the night. His parents loved him, but there was not too much money to go around. His father worked all the time; full-time job and a part-time job, too, while trying hard to support the fledging family. Now that Marcus was older, his mom had a part-time job, too.

Marcus entertained himself.

He was quite good at it. Especially in the summer when school was out.

Next year, he would be in fifth grade. Now, since it was summer break, he was simply curious.

Right now, the day was not too hot. Some clouds floated here and there and covered the sun and kept the heat at bay. Until past noon; that is, generally, when the burners kicked on. Summer in north Jersey on the outskirts of an old city.

No breeze, no movement.

It was a great day to be curious. To experiment with life. To find the obscure.

In a patch of spent turf that used to pretend to be grass, Marcus found some very small stones. Some stones were dark, some were light, some were round, and some were oval. Some of the stones were odd and some of the stones were even.

Marcus had a thought. He sat on the sidewalk in front of his house, took the stones and carefully made a line of the stones across the walkway in front of his house.

Then he returned and sat on his front stoop and watched. And waited.

A woman came hustling by, working hard to catch the bus in time. She glanced down and then over to Marcus and carefully stepped over the line of stones. She then continued on her way. She seemed busy and indifferent.

A middle-aged man with a newspaper under his arm walked down the sidewalk. He spotted the line of stones, stopped walking, toyed with one of the stones with the tip of his shoe, then shook his head and stepped over them with a long and exaggerated stride, and continued on his way. He seemed sad.

Marcus sat and watched.

A teenage girl on her bicycle did not even notice the line of stones. She plowed right through them as she pedaled her way to somewhere.

Oh, oh! The stones danced in all directions.

Marcus jumped up off the stoop. He quickly rescued the stones and, once more, arranged them into a careful line of stones across the sidewalk.

Gerald was the neighborhood tough guy. He was a handsome bully. Gerald caught the eye of all the girls.

At seventeen years of age, Gerald perceived himself to be the king of the neighborhood. Perception is not reality. Reality is a tricky thing.

Gerald walked down the sidewalk with the gorgeous Amanda on his arm. His muscles bulged under his clean white tee shirt and his ego burst like a thundercloud in August. They were heading to catch the bus for a date. Burgers, and a movie; afterwards, some passion. Gerald saw the stones. He stopped and looked over at Marcus sitting on the stoop. Gerald laughed with some drool and spittle emitting from the side of his mouth.

"Hey! Ya dopey kid! Did ya put these stones here?"

Amanda tugged on Gerald's arm. She pleaded a little as she glanced over at young Marcus.

"Ah, leave him alone, Gerald. He is just a kid. He is just playing."

"I asked you a question, punk. Answer me!" Gerald was bold and a bully. He ignored his gal.

Marcus was not afraid.

"I did."

"Why? Cuz, ya stupid?"

"Nah. To see what people would do. It is an experiment."

"Ha! Experiment this, punk!" Gerald kicked the stones with his high-top sneakers, tugged at Amanda, and dragged her on their way to the bus stop.

She turned and mouthed to Marcus, "I'm sorry."

Stone rescue time.

An elderly lady walked by with her walker. She was heading for the corner store for milk and bread.

She spotted the line of stones and promptly scolded Marcus for, "Making a tripping hazard."

Marcus jumped up, moved the stones, and then, when the elderly woman passed, he replaced them.

Mr. Simon Friedman taught science in high school for over forty years. In that same borough. He had now been retired for close to ten years; yet, his love for children and teaching remained strong. Mr. Friedman walked to the temple. Cane in hand.

Temple was just down the corner from where Marcus sat on the stoop.

Mr. Friedman was old now; every step was careful and calculated. Yet, he walked. He came across the line of stones; he waved his cane over them and he glanced over to Marcus and smiled.

A question.

"What is this line of stones for, young man?"

"It is an experiment."

"Ah. I love experiments. Did a few of them myself. Every experiment should have a purpose and then you learn. What is the purpose?"

"To see what people will do."

"And what did you learn?"

"Some people are sad. Some were mad. Some mean. Some ignore things."

Mr. Friedman smiled. One emotion was missing.

He dropped his cane and rather spryly jumped and danced over the line of stones, and smiled, and laughed, and waved his arms in the air like a silly duck flapping its wings, and he made funny faces.

Marcus laughed uproariously.

When he ran out of energy, Mr. Friedman picked up his cane and he laughed too and then asked, "Now. What did you learn, young man?"

"That some people are very happy and have fun over simple things. And when I am very old, I will laugh and dance and flap my arms like a duck in the air and act very silly. Because life is fun."

Mr. Friedman wiped tears away from his eyes and pointed the tip of his cane at Marcus and said, "Yes. Life is fun. That is a wonderful experiment, young man. Well, done."

Mr. Friedman went off to temple.

Marcus gathered up the line of stones.

There was a time long ago when the borough on the outskirts of the old city was innocent.

Nowadays, you have to search to find innocence.

It is still there.

The Branch Sitters

From: Flashes, Sparks, and Shorts: Flash Four

"I hit hard times, and you hit rocky times. As far as our hearts go, as far as our souls go—we never really left each other, but we drifted apart. It was meant to be and only makes this reunion even more meaningful. And there were those days when we thought we would live forever, and there were those days when we were young, full of life, and everything shone, even in our worst times and our worse days. Now, it is all gone. Faded away within the eclipse of time."

It was a mighty oak tree. Massive. Its roots went from Sussex County, New Jersey to near Perth, Australia.

Exaggeration, of course, but it was a massive oak.

It had one branch that seemed to go on forever; powerful, thick, strong, and forever. It pointed west and looked over the fields of corn.

His father, the old farmer, tied a rope swing with a finished and polished seat of maple wood to that branch. Two holes drilled on each end and the rope and knots passed between.

The two of them enjoyed that swing more than vanilla ice cream on a July afternoon.

Well, maybe not. An exaggeration. Vanilla ice cream is amazing.

Maddie (Madeline), lived on the neighboring farm. Cute

as a button. Twelve years old. Sparkling blue eyes. Long blonde hair woven in a pigtail that wandered down her back. She wore a yellow dress with red straps that hitched with two big red buttons in the front of the dress. She wore pink socks with teddy bears along the top of them. Open-toed shoes because she was so proud of those socks.

Chad (Chadwick) was thirteen. Long hair like a mop. Brown with hints of red highlights. Handsome and strong for his age. He wore a tee shirt with the New York Yankees logo on it. His favorite team. Baseball. His love; but not his only love. Oh, no! For sure, not his only love.

He wore black shorts and canvas sneakers.

His baseball glove, a baseball, and his wooden bat sat on the ground underneath the swing. Her doll was next to it. Little Lulu was the doll's name. She was a mermaid; yellow hair and green fins.

They sat on the branch watching the late August sunset over the fields.

She confessed as her hand crawled into his hand and their fingers interlocked, "I could sit here forever. But only with you."

He took her hand and confessed, "I could sit here, too. Forever. But only with you, too."

Surprise! Oh, no! His father's words shook them to the core. The old farmer!

"Chadwick! What on earth are you two doing up there?"

"We are branch sitters, Dad."

"Okay. No! That is not okay, because I do not know what that means! You could fall and get hurt! Break your necks. How did you get up there?"

The boy confessed to his father. He was honest and truthful.

"We climbed up the rope from the swing."

"Well, get down now!"

They did so. Chad helped Maddie down the rope. He turned his head so as not to, by accident, look up her dress. He might have failed and caught a glimpse. Teddy bear underwear. He had failed on the way up and failed on the way down, too.

The old farmer was not happy. Maddie took Little Lulu and ran all the way home.

Now, all these years later, the oak tree was even more massive. Quiet power. Immeasurable.

This tree laughed at lightning strikes, and wind, and rain and ice storms and blizzards. It was forever.

He sat on the branch and recalled all that had passed. His father's funeral shook him to the core. The late October sky and the sunset in front of him that was full of blues, oranges, and muted reds captivated him, but he could not hold back the tears. The old rope swing was gone; rotted away with time. To gain access to the branch, he used a ladder that he borrowed from the barn.

He now owned all this land. This farm. What would he do with it? He had joined the United States Navy after Maddie got married. He fled New Jersey.

Fled, in tears at who and what he let slip away.

Now, after twenty years at sea, and on land, he returned. To this.

His father was gone. So was his mother. And there was Maddie at the funeral. Just as beautiful as she always was. His career worked out; her marriage did not.

Those were rocky times. Time is an enemy and an ally; all at the same time.

He heard her climb the ladder. He turned and watched

her do so. Long blonde hair; not in a ponytail. Just long and wavy and tumbling across her beautiful soul and body. Her blue eyes sparkled as she bent down and carefully crawled hand-over-hand across the branch. She wore the same dress that she wore at the funeral. Black. Hugged her curves. Maddie's copious breasts hung out of the dress as she crawled along the branch. Westward. Maddie made no effort to hide them. She was barefoot.

She left her shoes at the base of the ladder.

"Careful, Maddie," Chad warned. He added, "We are not so young anymore."

Maddie said, "I knew that I would find you here."

Once seated, her hand crawled across the branch and she felt for his hand. They clasped hands. They held hands in love and they treasured the gentle bond. It had been too long since they were branch sitters. Together.

Maddie spoke first. Chad answered.

"Confession. I missed you."

"Confession here, too. I missed you more."

"Tie. I almost expect your dad to come along and yell at us to climb down."

Chad smiled and replied.

"Me, too. Sorry your marriage did not work out. I must say that you look gorgeous. Thank you for coming to his funeral."

"I would not miss it. I have to say . . . I love you."

"I love you, too Forever. Let's just sit here until dark. Until the sun dips over that cornfield. Then we can be together. Forever."

"Confession time! I have to ask . . . all those years ago, did you look up my dress when I climbed that rope?"

"I did. Teddy bears."

"Ha! Thank you. I guess that I always knew that. I still wear them. Do you want to look up it . . . forever?"

"Forever."

"We hit hard times, Chad. Are these the good times?"

"They are, Maddie. Please, this might be an awful place for a marriage proposal but, will you marry me?"

"Are you kidding? This is the perfect place. Our special place. I will. Yes! I have waited. So long. Too long."

"Too long. Thank you."

They kissed while the sun dipped below the horizon and over the cornfields. It was a glorious kiss, and it shook their souls to the core.

After the kiss, Maddie said, "I could sit here forever. But only with you."

"We will. Forever."

The remaining sunlight kissed them both within the eclipse of time.

It was a mighty oak tree. Massive. Its roots went from Sussex County, New Jersey to near Perth, Australia.

And there they sat. On the branch facing west. Looking over the cornfields.

This tree laughed at lightning strikes, and wind, and rain and ice storms and blizzards. It was forever.

So were they. In love. Forever.

Branch sitters.

A Quiz on a Random Benjamin Franklin Appearances

From: Flashes, Sparks, and Shorts: Flash Four

On Independence Day just before midnight, if Mr. Benjamin Franklin randomly shows up at the front door of your home in New Jersey and knocks on your door and asks you if you want a pint of beer because God loves you and beer is proof, you should:

A: Immediately take the pint of beer and down it in one or two gulps.

B: Go inside the house, find your Bible, and ask Mr. Franklin to show you the verse that proves that fact about God and beer.

C: Ask Mr. Franklin if he needs a kite and a key.

D: Stop being so cheap and upgrade to a better quality of Scotch whiskey that does not cause hallucinatory behavior.

E: See if Mr. Franklin will sign your replica copy of the Declaration of Independence. For no charge.

D: Shout, "We must, indeed, all hang together or, most assuredly, we shall all hang separately!" Show him his image on a one-hundred-dollar bill, then close the front door, and then go back to bed.

E: Ask Mr. Franklin if he needs to mail a letter, or if he requires a document printed, even if you do not have a printing press in your home. After all, Franklin was a printer, and he was a postmaster, too.

F: Check for proper local laws, taxes, permits, and licenses required for historical Founding Fathers of the United States of America peddling pints of beer at the front doors of homes. This is New Jersey and chances are that Mr. Franklin has unwittingly run afoul of the local laws. Nowadays there is a permit, tax, and license for everything.

G: All of the above.

A Somewhat Correct Answer

G: All of the above

The Owl in the Cemetery

From: Flashes, Sparks, and Shorts: Flash Four

Life and the adventures within sure are a mystery.

Sometimes, there are calls to our soul out of the night. In the early morning. Out of the darkness; to find a new path. A new journey. Where are we going? Should we go together? Should we go alone? Should we just go?

Just another Monday.

Ten minutes to five in the morning. June weather arrived and even at this time of the morning, it was already hot. He did not run the air-conditioning in the truck; just rolling down the windows sufficed.

Later, during the flip-flop back to home, it would be air-conditioning time.

He glided the truck to a stop at the red traffic light at the four-way intersection. A major intersection in these parts. Thousands of souls travel on these roads each day.

Gas station in front of him. The cemetery to his right. Dead ahead, was the open road, to the left, a curve and then the open road.

He had ridden this same way to work for over fourteen years. At first, he loved his job. Now, it was a chore. It was no longer fun; however, the end was near. He clicked off the time until retirement.

Nowadays, these young employees no longer cared, no longer listened and even though, in theory, he was the boss; they considered him old and dumb, and they knew everything. He kept things on the rails and picked up the slack on his own and bided his time. In a few years, it would not be his concern.

They all had their chance to learn from his years of wisdom and his experiences. Now, they could learn on their own.

Honestly, he stopped trying; stopped caring; stopped mentoring; and he gave up a few years ago. The company kept him around because of what he did know and the fact that no one else, especially these young bucks, wanted to come into work at five in the morning. Each day. Every day. Not for a few days. Or a few weeks. For years and years. The company was lucky when the young bucks even showed up for work. Forget about being on time.

Red light. Wait. It was a long wait time.

The echo of the call came clearly across the cemetery to his open window.

"Whoooo, whooo, whoooooo."

A lonely yet enthralling call out of the darkness. Who was listening?

It caught his attention. Loud and clear. An owl in a tree in the cemetery. Once again, the owl called out into the early morning darkness.

"Whoooo, whooo, whoooooo."

Green light. He stepped on the gas pedal of the truck and thought about how he never heard an owl call from there before. That owl has found a tree to call home.

Tuesday morning. Same traffic light. Red again.

"Whoooo, whooo, whoooooo."

Loud and clear, once again.

Wednesday and Thursday were the same. The owl in the cemetery, in his home, making his calls to the world. To anyone listening. There seemed to be only a few listening. Maybe only one human.

It seemed as if the owl called out for a reason; for a purpose.

The man in the truck felt the call.

After listening to the owl's call on Thursday morning, by Thursday afternoon, the man in the truck had a plan. He was usually up by three in the morning, anyway. He wanted to see this glorious, yet lonely creature for himself. Find his home. His tree. Decipher the mission of the owl.

It was a moonless night and morning. Dark. It was now Friday.

He parked his truck in the entrance driveway to the cemetery. Technically, the sacred ground did not open the gates until dawn. No one would mind his violation of the rules. He was respectful and stayed on the main path. Armed with a flashlight, he made his way to the center of the cemetery, on the main drive lane.

Click. Off went the light. No distractions. Silence amongst the resting souls on the holy grounds. All those lifetimes.

Respect. All those missions.

And he stopped and stood in an area where he thought he strategically could hear the lonely call.

His wait earned a quick reward.

"Whoooo, whooo, whoooooo."

"Whoooo, whooo, whoooooo."

The man quickly spun around, flipped his flashlight on, and went off in the direction of the call.

"Whoooo, whooo, whoooooo."

The owl in the cemetery called out as if it was meant for discovery. Meant to provide direction.

It was a majestic and sprawling oak tree. Embedded deep in the roots of the world. Established. Limbs that pointed to Heaven in the darkness. The home of the owl in the cemetery. He tried to flip off the flashlight in time; but his efforts were too late.

There was a flap of the wings and just a glimpse of the majesty of the owl upon a backdrop with just enough of a hint of light to be able to detect the owl's magnificence.

The owl had revealed his lair; his wisdom, and his secrets. The man in the truck sought them all, and he found them all, too.

The man's flashlight caught a glimpse of a nearby headstone.

With the aid of the flashlight, he read the headstone of the grave that positioned itself beneath the majesty of the oak tree.

"Marvin Anderson,"

"Born August 09, 1934. Died: December 12, 2016."

" A teacher. He dedicated his life to imparting wisdom to his students. Because wisdom is more precious than gold is."

The man in the truck now knew the purpose of this mission. Of the owl in the cemetery. Of the call.

Wisdom.

He flipped the flashlight off and walked out of the darkness into the light. Renewal of the soul is an amazing thing. Sometimes, all it takes is a call.

"Gather around now, men. Come on over here. Let me

teach you what is happening here in the chiller plant today. You don't see these troubles too often. It is very complex. I can show you. Please remember this event. This is a very valuable lesson."

Sometimes, there are calls to our soul out of the night. In the early morning. Out of the darkness; to find a new path.

A new journey.

Life and the adventures within sure are a mystery.

Specifics

From: Flashes, Sparks, and Shorts: Flash Four

He always felt as if he was a fair and logical man. Worked his way up the corporate ladder to an executive director position in a large accounting corporation. Now, with retirement looming, he had some doubts if he should put his retirement papers in sooner than later.

"Darlene, when you have a chance, can you please see me in my office? I want to go over this report draft for the Winkler account," the executive said to his "daily work partner."

He had received a reprimand a few weeks ago when Darlene complained to the human resources department that the executive referred to her as his assistant. That made her feel "subjected" to the executive. She felt offended and unhappy.

They settled on a specific new job title that made Darlene happy. The executive went along with the new title. Years ago, when he was a young executive, they assigned the title of secretary to Darlene's position.

Whatever. All these specifics were wearisome.

Nowadays, everyone is addicted to being offended.

The two of them went over the changes to the draft text while Dalene intermittently played with her cellphone and chewed and cracked gum in her mouth.

"Okay, can you have these changes completed by this

afternoon, Darlene?"

She looked at the screen on her cellphone to check the time.

Wristwatches were a thing of the past. It was eleven in the morning.

"Define this afternoon? I mean, give me a specific time this afternoon."

"Ah, three o'clock."

"No can do. Another time? A specific time."

The executive sat back in his chair and sighed. All these specifics were wearisome.

"I will defer to you for the specific time."

"Four-eighteen."

"All righty now. That works. Very specific, indeed. Thank you."

The text from his wife came through on his cellphone just before lunchtime.

Wife: **'Please stop at the food store on the way home. I need strawberry shortcake frosting and a vanilla cake mix. For Patty's b-day party. Thanks.'**

He replied: **'Ok.'**

"Could you please tell me where the cake frosting and cake mix are in the store?" The executive asked the store clerk stocking the shelves in the dairy aisle.

The young man stood up, nodded his head, and mumbled, "Yes."

Then he went back to stocking the shelf full of milk.

Puzzled, the executive said, "Well, ah, well, where is it? Please."

The store clerk stopped stocking the shelf and turned to

the executive and said, "Where is it? In aisle three. Halfway down the aisle on the right as you face the store. Initially," he blinked a little, and then continued, "you asked me if I could tell you where the items are located. I answered you specifically with yes because you didn't ask me where they were, only if I could tell you where they were. Specifics are important. There are thousands of products in this store."

He went back to stocking the shelf.

"Thanks. I think."

All these specifics were wearisome.

"Honey, this is not the cake mix that I usually buy. I always get the Rosy Butt-Cheeks brand."

"Oh. I will go back and switch it. We want everyone to enjoy rosy butt-cheeks at this party. I know that specifics are important. Been learning that."

"They are."

He was not going to mention that her text did not specify an exact brand to purchase.

"I have to pick up a file at the office. I will switch the cake mix and then go to the office and be back soon."

"Okay. Specifically, what exact time? I have to make dinner."

He sighed and said, "Seven-fifteen."

Old Mel had been the night housekeeper on the accounting firm's floor in the high-rise for as long as the executive could remember. They always chatted whenever the executive got stuck working late. Old Mel was dusting cubicle walls and file cabinets when the executive walked by him.

"Hey, Mr. Turner. How ya been? Have not seen ya working late for a while. I guess that is a good thing."

"It is, Mel. I am all right. You?"

Mel smiled and said, "Great. Job security here with this dust."

The executive had a thought.

"Say, Mel. Let me ask you. Please. When you dust, do you target an exact area? As in specific dusty spots or specific dust particles?"

Mel screwed his face up and held his duster in the air while clearly confused by the questions.

"Huh? Ya stop off at Shakey's for a few of them Manhattans that ya like, Mr. Turner?"

Mr. Turner laughed and replied, "No. I wish. Seriously. I know it is weird to ask, but everyone these days is so into specifics and exact details. They are so illogical. It is freaking me out."

Mel nodded and took his duster and swept it over the top of the file cabinet.

After he gave the top of the cabinet a good sweep, Mel smiled and said, "I get-cha now. Yup. Lots of whackos around these days. Nah. I just pick up all the dust equally. It all pays the same. Big dust. Little dust. Otherwise, I will be here forever. Ain't into specifics. All that exacting bullshit is wearisome. I just get my job done and go the hell home and drink beer and watch the ballgame."

Mr. Turner smiled widely and said, "Finally. Logic. Thanks, Mel. You made my day. See you soon."

"See ya, Mr. Turner."

The next day, Mr. Turner wrote his retirement letter to his executive vice president and copied the executive management chain. He gave them his retirement date. Six months of notice. He had decided that this all was past him now. Too wearisome. Maybe he would get a part-time cleaning job and work with old Mel. Mel was the only one around here who made any sense and who was not a nutcase.

One hour later, after submitting his retirement notice, the executive vice president sent him an email reply. The executive vice president copied all the executive management chains of command on the message. An entire group of confused and dazed executives. Mr. Turner clicked on the message and read it aloud to his office walls. He had a feeling it was going to confirm specifically and exactly why he needed to pack it in.

"I received your retirement letter. Thank you for the six months of notice. Congratulations. You will be difficult, if not impossible, to replace. One item that we need to complete for your file records. Please, can specify the exact time of the day that you will officially retire on the date of January 3rd? Specially. Exactly. Thank you."

Yes, indeed, this is why he needed to pack it all in. All these specifics. Mr. Turner sighed.

He typed out the answer:

"Seven-eleven, P.M."

He might as well pick a lucky number to go out on.

All these specifics were so wearisome.

Old Mel was correct. It all pays the same. Just get the job done and go the hell home and drink beer and watch the ballgame.

Today Is Your Lucky Day

From: Flashes, Sparks, and Shorts: Flash Four

It was a humdrum sort of Saturday.

One of those days where he could not get any traction on any of the projects that he planned for, or his wife wanted done around the house. It was raining, so cutting the grass was out of the question. As was also due to the rain—scraping and painting the kitchen windows. He forgot to bring home the basin wrench from the shop, therefore replacing the kitchen sink faucet was also a no-go.

He was not going to waste money by purchasing another wrench when he already had one. You just don't use them often enough.

"I made coffee, but we ran out of milk." His wife announced just as he returned from walking the dog. In the pouring rain.

"I will go to the supermarket for a gallon. Let me towel off Mr. Pee-A lot and I will go."

"Okay. Get a quart. A gallon always goes bad before we use it up. Ever since you stopped eating Fruity Blob-Ohs cereal and not using milk much anymore."

He put his hat and jacket on, grabbed his car keys and as he pulled the backdoor open to leave, he said, "They have a weird aftertaste. Be right back."

The supermarket was right down the road from their home. Two lefts, one right and you could glide into the parking lot. The rain had let up a little, but he still hustled into the front door of the store.

He jumped in surprise as the sliding door opened and he walked into the supermarket. Balloons and confetti exploded in the air all around him! A foghorn went off! Store employees were shouting, cheering, and screaming at him, blowing the little horn sounders that you blow in celebration at a birthday party as they hurled paper confetti in the air all around him.

It was bedlam, and the man nearly jumped out of his shoes.

Then he stood, shocked, and in surprise as flashbulbs went off all around him. Other shoppers in the store gathered around the mayhem to see what had happened.

"Congratulations, sir!"

A man shouted at the befuddled shopper.

The shouting man dressed in a shirt and tie, with a pencil-thin mustache that looked as if someone drew it on his face with a marker, and with just a blob of two or three long hairs on the front of his otherwise bald head.

Pencil-thin mustache man continued to explain.

"Today is your lucky day. You are the five-hundredth shopper today at You Really Do Not Save supermarket! And you have won a free one-hundred-dollar shopping spree!"

More cheers! More clapping! More horns and balloons and confetti! Pencil-thin mustache man rushed in to shake his hand and suddenly, other store employees shoved clipboards with papers on them at the man, who still stood there in shock.

"I am Mr. Whisker Looney . . . the store manager here at store number 076760. Here is your free shopper card.

There are just a few forms for you to sign before you can shop for free."

Mr. Looney nodded at the first employee, who handed the first paper on a clipboard and a pen to the startled man.

"Please read and sign this form. It agrees to our store taking your photo and your name and address and using it on our website. Be sure to include your email address so we can spam you with endless emails every day for years and years."

The man completed and signed the form. Then another clipboard appeared.

"This form agrees that you never sue our store if you slip and fall on your ass in one of our aisles while shopping. Legal stuff. Tricky banana peels and such."

He signed that form and another clipboard immediately appeared.

"Sign this one, too. It agrees to the terms of the free shopping spree. No alcohol. No dairy products. No meat. The free shopping spree does not include fresh fruits and vegetables or laundry detergent."

The shocked man looked up and asked, "No laundry detergent? That is rather random, Mr. Looney."

"It is. Hey, I didn't make this bullshit promotional up. Corporate nonsense. But you can take up to fifty boxes of Fruity Blob-Ohs cereal."

"No, thanks. They have a weird aftertaste."

"Yup. Sure, do. That's why we are trying to dump them on you. Can't even give 'em away. Anyway, just sign the form and we have one last requirement before you can shop your ass off! Just don't fall on it!"

"Fall on what? My ass or the banana peel?"

"Both. Just sign."

He signed it. The store employees all took their clipboards and fled. The crowd scattered and only a photographer remained; snapping away; photograph after photograph.

"What is the last requirement?" The man asked.

"You have to do ten jumping jacks."

"HUH?"

"Yup. Ten of them."

"What if I was a ninety-year-old man?"

"Well, that was the last-second corporate gotcha to get out of giving away the free stuff, but ya ain't, so do the stupid jumping jacks and I can go to lunch."

"This is the craziest free thing that ain't really free that I have ever seen or heard of!"

"I agree. Corporate bullshit."

The man did his jumping jacks; Mr. Looney shook his hand. They smiled for one last picture and Mr. Looney took off for lunch.

"Honey, I need a hand with the groceries," the man side to his wife as he walked in the back door.

"Groceries? You have been gone forever. You went for a quart of milk."

"Yes, I did. Which, by the way, I did not get. Mr. Looney made it very clear that the store did not include any dairy products in the free shopping spree. Here . . . stand by the door. I will hand you the bags. It is raining like crazy out here."

"Free, shopping spree? What? No dairy products? Who the hell is Mr. Looney? Who has a name like that?"

"It is a very long story."

It was a humdrum sort of Saturday.

Sort of.

Mr. Ebenezer Scrooge's Resume

From: A Bowl Full of Marbles. Flashes, Sparks, and Shorts: Flash Five

Objective: To obtain a part-time position promoting Christmas, and hope, joy, and love.

Attributes: Learns well from mistakes. Good with ghosts and things that go bump in the night. Superior money counting skills. Loves and honors Christmas and the holiday season.

Education: Graduated with honors from a remote boarding school when Senior Scrooge (father) shipped me off there in exile.

Experience: Apprenticed in money lending and trades and such from working with Old Fezziwig. Taught the value of money, taught nuances of business and respecting others, taught about hard work, Christmas parties, drinking porter, dancing, being jovial and happy. How to be glorious. Fell in love.

Career: Forgot how to be glorious. No longer danced. No longer jovial. Worshipped money and power. Ditched love. Forgot every lesson learned from Old Fezziwig.

Met Jacob Marley. Went into business with Mr. Marley. Opened money lending and trading firm.

Co-Owner-Partner: Scrooge and Marley for over 40 years.

Connived, cheated, became evil and very rich.

Dined in melancholy taverns.

Marley died, and I inherited the company and everything associated with it.

Became an evil-money-grubbing miser. Continued legacy of cheating, conniving, and being grumpy and evil. Treated everyone, including my employee(s) very poorly and was very happy to do so.

Despised Christmas and laughter and my only living family member.

Counted money for fun.

Jacob Marley was my only friend and after he died, I had no other friends and only spoke of business and how to make money and cheat, connive, and become wealthier and wealthier.

Had an amazing encounter with four ghosts (Yes. Technically, there were four ghosts. Despite rumors, and non-factual testimonies of only three ghosts) on the Christmas Eve anniversary of my old partner's death. In fact, Jacob Marley returned to visit me as the "Head Ghost." Not sure if it was undigested beef, or some moldy cheese, or a dab of mustard, or an underdone potato, but there were ghosts.

I am quite sure of it; and you will not get me to change my mind or my testimony.

Changed my ways.

Realized the importance of family.

Became very, very happy.

Remembered how to dance and how to love.

Tiny Tim lived because I paid for the best doctors and the best medical care for him.

Realized life is very, very short; make the most of it.

Dined in happy pubs.

Loved everything about Christmas and life.

Became glorious again.

Summary: Give me a chance. I will teach you about Christmas, and love, joy, and hope. Will teach you how to love life and be glorious. Will work for no charge. I do not need the money.

And be happy to do so.

God bless us. Everyone.

Corporate Confusion

From: A Bowl Full of Marbles. Flashes, Sparks, and Shorts: Flash Five

Mr. Dwayne DeMercotroit was the big boss. His title was Executive Director of, well, something or other. Yet, no one actually knew what his title was, or exactly what he did at the Whiz-Bang Corporation.

Dwayne was tall, and very thin, and he had eyebrows like two leaping caterpillars. He wore his hair short, yet his hair stood on end. His face looked as if he was perpetually walking into an eighty-miles-per-hour windstorm. Squinty eyes and a pushed-in face.

Dwayne had a fancy corner office on the ninth floor of the corporate headquarters. The tenth floor housed the super-demi-god executive suite. Dwayne was one level below the demi-gods, but his goal was to land on the tenth floor someday.

His administrative assistant sat outside of Dwayne's office, but the telephone on her desk never rang. She never worked on her computer. The monitor was off. She did not have any pens, or pencils, or papers on her desk. There was not even a file cabinet in her cubicle. Mostly, she simply sat there and waited for something to happen. And checked her lipstick.

Mr. DeMercotroit always wore a suit and necktie that was too short, and a plaid jacket, with black shoes that squeaked when he walked up and down the hallways of the massive corporate headquarters. And Dwayne always walked around, squinting, and staring at fellow employees, while carrying a coffee cup in one hand and a manila folder in the other hand.

Dwayne mentioned that he served in the military. But he never said what branch, or when, or what he did, or where. He told everyone that he graduated with a master's degree in something, from Blabbo University, but no one ever heard of that institute of higher learning. His undergraduate degree came from Philanderer College in Maple Syrupville, Vermont. No one ever heard of that college or location, either. Dwayne also played professional baseball; had a tryout with a professional basketball team, but had to quit because of a twisted ankle. He swam the English Channel twice and scaled Pike's Peak once.

Only once.

Dwayne said he was going to scale it twice, but it was easier than he thought, so he never gave it a second try.

Because it was too costly and confusing, the Human Resources Department at the Whiz-Bag Corporation did very limited background checks on their hires. . ..

Frankie Fankenhauser worked in the mailroom at the corporate headquarters. A summer temp job. He just graduated high school. Until he started college in the fall of this year, this was a outstanding summer job for him. Frankie was going to be a business major, so this little jaunt in a major corporation would provide some valuable insight into the corporate world. He needed to save up money for a car for college.

Frankie stood in front of the desk of Mr. DeMercotroit's administrative assistant.

She looked up at him and smiled.

"How can I help you?"

"Hello. I am Frankie Frankenhauser. I have an appointment with Mr. DeMercotroit for ten this morning."

She shrugged her shoulders, looked at her watch and said, "That's a lot of Franks. I know nothing about it. But it is one minute to ten. You are very prompt. Go right in."

Frankie nervously knocked on the open door of the office of the big super-chief. He was not sure what he did wrong! Maybe he miss-delivered some important mail?

Mr. DeMercotroit bellowed from behind his desk, and he stood up and waved.

His caterpillar eyebrows flapped like windshield wipers in a thunderstorm as he spoke.

"Come right in! Sit down here in the guest chair, Frankfurter! Sit down. Notice my plush carpet, the fantastic elegant furnishings, and the fancy executive office I have here!"

Frankie crept slowly into the office, as he looked all around.

As he carefully sunk into the guest chair, and the big boss sat in his high-back executive chair, Frankie sputtered out some words.

"It is very nice. Beautiful office, sir. However, my name is Frankie Frankenhauser. Not Frankfurter."

Mr. DeMercotroit waved dismissively and said, "Oh well, whatever. That's a lot of Franks."

"Have I done something wrong, sir?"

"Frankly . . . get it?"

"Yes, I get it, sir."

"Frankly, yes! I have been putting it off for weeks and weeks to meet with you," Mr. DeMercotroit said, as he then placed his hands on top of a pile of at least one-hundred manila folders, "I have your file in here somewhere. I have to file all of these, but never take care of it, but I have noticed how you procrastinate terribly in your job duties and are not efficient at all!"

Frankie screwed his face up and stared at the big boss.

"I do? I mean, I sort and deliver mail. My supervisor never complains about my work. I am a temp in the mailroom for the summer."

"Exactly! All I ever see you do is walk around here with mail and packages in your hands and deliver them to offices, while you roll a mail cart up and down the hallways!"

"Ah, yes, that is my job, sir."

Mr. DeMercotroit screwed his face up like a corkscrew and asked, "It is?"

"Yes, sir."

Mr. DeMercotroit pounded his desk with his fist and stood up.

"Well, now. That settles that. Keep up the good work! Come on over here, Frankenfurter. Let me show you this photograph of Pikes Peak. I scaled that sucker with my bare hands while wearing some baseball spikes, and was going to climb it again, but. . .."

Later that day, on his lunch break, Frankie called his father.

"Dad, I have been thinking. I changed my mind. Instead of college, I want to go to trade school. Plumbing. Work with you. Take over Frankenhauser Plumbing and Heating, someday when you retire. The family business. I am thinking that this corporate business world might not be for me."

Lungs Like a Blowtorch

From: A Bowl Full of Marbles. Flashes, Sparks, and Shorts: Flash Five

Ah, yes, the nostalgia. It tends to stay with you in a very special way. Longing for the way that things used to be in such simpler times.

"Timmmmmyyy! Ariannnnna!"

The call beckoned throughout the neighborhood. Through an open upstairs window. Hands cupped around her mouth. Mother Esposito took another deep breath and once again launched into the call.

"Time for dinnnnnerrrrr!"

Mother Esposito was rather large, and she had lungs like a blowtorch.

There were no cellphones. No internet. No texting. There were simpler and better ways of communicating.

Old city neighborhoods are very special and so unique. The nuances that they have are more than intriguing. They captivate.

This old city neighborhood had it all. From Goldberg's Jewish Delicatessen on the corner of North 12th Street and Belmont Avenue, serving up that golden mustard on top of the hot pastrami, to the German Pork Store, to the Campus Sweet Shop, to Gabby's Cabin, it was all diverse and special and unique. Unless you grew up there; it was very difficult to describe to a person that did not experience it. And the nuances of growing up there stick in your mind forever.

It was only three weeks after Christmas. January. The longest month with approximately three-hundred-and eighty-four days. Or thereabouts.

It was a bitter cold Wednesday, and overnight, there had been about six inches or thereabouts of snow. Unlike these days; no media-induced panic occurred. No one hid under their kitchen table in fear over a few inches of snow.

Work continued. School was open; just a normal day. The stores were all open, including the supermarkets and the shelves, all stocked with the normal numbers of products and goods. The mailman and the milkman all delivered their goods and made the rounds. The city buses all ran. The world revolved normally.

The city snowplows came barging through and made the streets slightly cavernous; but that was part of the silent, snowy magic.

He lived in the small house right next door to the Esposito's house. He was a devoted husband and father to two children. Off he went to work at his same time. When hearing of the forecast, he set his alarm for an hour and a half early. He needed to get up early to allow for the snow. His shift at the machine shop started at six in the morning. That three-thirty alarm was hell, but up he was. Hat, overcoat, gloves, scarf, and boots. Snow shovel in hand; shovel the driveway and front sidewalk while he warmed up the old car, load some bags of sand in the trunk for weight, chains on the wheels, and off to work he went. No allowance for calling out of work! No excuses. This was the day and age of commitment; not the time to be a cupcake.

Off the kiddies went to school, like teetering penguins making their stiff way along the snowy terrain. Sledding, and snowball fights, and snowmen, and fun!

By three in the afternoon, the snowstorm was almost a memory. Only the lingering snow piles on the edges of life and the roads and sidewalks remained as a testimony to its passing through. The kiddies went in reverse and trudged home. There was homework to do but there was also sledding, and snowball fights, and snowmen and fun! The father made his way back home after the shift ended, along what were now mostly clear streets. Just some patches of ice and snow here and there.

The Esposito's house was small. Narrow, but two stories tall with a basement below. A wooden porch with stone steps. The bedrooms were on the upper floor. Kitchen, dining room, living room on the first floor. One bathroom upstairs. The home sat in a most unusual location. Next to an old restaurant; they shared a common driveway. Just off a city side street. If the home was a thousand square feet, that was an exaggeration. The Esposito family were a New Jersey-Italian family. Catholic and proud to be so. They went to mass most every morning at Saint Gerard's parish. The children attended Saint Gerard's Parochial School. Father, mother, grandfather, grandmother, and two children. All in one-thousand square feet of city living. When Grandma (Nonna) Esposito slow-simmered her gravy on Sundays and Wednesdays for her pasta dishes, you could smell the heavenly aroma for two city blocks. A luxury was a color television in the living room. They always gathered around the set and watched Lawrence Welk on Saturday evenings.

This snowy evening was Wednesday, and it was the traditional spaghetti dinner night. You could not smell Nonna Esposito's gravy slow-simmering throughout the neighborhood on this snowy evening. They kept the windows closed tightly and the glorious aromas could not escape.

The father pulled into the driveway and shut off the engine. He grabbed his lunch pail and headed for the back door.

The father burst in through the back door of the home and it was cozy and warm and it was inviting. It was now four-thirty in the afternoon. He had left the home around twelve hours earlier. A long day. To say the least.

Yet, he felt wonderful. The kitchen table was set; his beer mug had a cold beer poured in it; his newspaper sat next to his place. An old table radio on a shelf played some easy listening music from a local radio station. His wife kissed his cheek and waved to his seat at the head of the table. She had done her hair up and had some gentle perfume on. The mother of this family was very lovely.

"Sit down, honey. Relax now. Have your beer. How was your day? You must be starving!"

"I am, baby. Ah, ya know. The bosses are on our asses. After the Christmas shutdown. We gotta make those numbers! Production. What's for dinner? Smells great!"

"I defrosted the leftover turkey from Christmas and New Year's Day. Turkey soup, some white meat, some dark meat. Stuffing, green beans, and salad and your beer. I even got your pickled onions."

Nothing went to waste in those days.

"Ya the best."

The father took a sip of beer and he grabbed his newspaper and started to read it. Had to check the hockey scores from last night.

"Where are the kids? They ain't gonna be late for dinner. Are they?"

The mother smiled. She knew. It was Wednesday.

"Oh no. They came home and did their homework and then went to the vacant lot with their sleds to sled down the plowed snow piles."

The father looked precariously over the edge of his

newspaper at his wife, as his wife added, "They went with the Esposito kids."

He nodded and went back to his beer and the hockey scores.

From behind the newspaper, the father said, "Okay. Mother Esposito will call them all home any minute now. That woman has lungs like a blowtorch."

Almost on queue; above the easy listening music, the call went out from the Esposito's house.

"Timmmmmyyy! Adriannnnna!"

The call beckoned throughout the neighborhood. Through an open upstairs window. Hands cupped around her mouth. Mother Esposito took another deep breath and once again launched into the call.

"Time for dinnnnnerrrrr!"

Mother Esposito was rather large, and, indeed, she had lungs like a blowtorch.

A few minutes later, their children burst through the door—red-faced and cold, but that turkey soup and dinner would do the trick.

Old city neighborhoods are very special and so unique. The nuances that they have are more than intriguing. They captivate.

They tend to stay with you forever.

The Sunday that the Bell Fell

From: A Bowl Full of Marbles. Flashes, Sparks, and Shorts: Flash Five

The Worsley family had overseen the ringing of the church bell for as long as most of the parishioners of the little church recalled. At the Call to Worship and after the Recessional and the Benediction, one of the family members, rang the church bell in the tower. Ten tugs on the rope that wound its way from the bell tower to behind the Altar.

Ring that bell; proclaim God's glory for a mile or so. Give or take, depending upon how clear the air was, to carry the sound through the noise of the world.

The family alternated the bell-ringers on a rotational basis through the family members. First, it was Chuck, then Shawn, then Nadia, and then Sharon. If it was a special holiday service, then often, they all would ring the bell together. No one was sure how it began with the Worsley family taking the role of the official bell-ringers for the church, but the tradition continued forever.

It was a small church; a heavy oak wood interior full of dark finishes. Glorious stained-glass windows lined each side of the sanctuary. The Altar area had a Lectern and a Pulpit, and the Pastor Bench, and the choir sat behind them in rows of robed musical aspirations. An education building attached to the sanctuary at a right angle, and the basement had a fellowship hall and a small kitchen.

All under the control of God's glory.

Pastor Lumpkin had been the pastor at the church for over twenty years. He was quite short and diminutive in stature. In fact, he used a box behind the Pulpit to lift himself up the microphone. Everyone knew the good pastor for his kindness; Hellfire and Brimstone were not in his sermon mixtures. However, he tended to be a bit long-winded in the Pulpit. Not boring, that would be too harsh for Christians to say to describe Pastor Lumpkin's sermons. Long-winded was a kinder term.

He seemed to be especially long-winded when there was a big sporting event on television and radio at one in the afternoon.

The young father sat in the first pew on the left side of the sanctuary. Often, his little son sat next to him. The boy was well-behaved for a three-year-old. The young father oversaw audio taping the worship services for the shut-ins of the congregation. Sitting where he did, allowed him access to a side door, which led to a room where they kept the audio recording equipment contained. The young father often had to tend to the tapes and equipment; therefore, worshippers grew accustomed to him getting up and down during the service. He did so silently and gracefully. Even while towing his son along, too.

One Sunday in spring, right after Easter. . ..

The Yankees played the Red Sox at one in the afternoon. It was an early season match-up of rivals.

Pastor Lumpkin was grasping at sermon straws to find the enthralling words to fit the time when Easter was over and Satan defeated. The sermon rambled on and on, like a freight train at a railroad crossing when you must use the bathroom. Occasionally, in the long string of cars, a freight car passes by that is colorful or has some interesting graffiti on it or some inventive painted obscenities; however, most of the experience is bores-ville.

The Yankees fans in the congregation kept checking their watches. And one Red Sox fan, too.

And Mrs. Tudley, who had a Sunday roast in the oven.

Just when Pastor Lumpkin was running out of Acts of the Apostles, he pulled the ultimate sermon straw out of the pack. For some reason, lost to time, Pastor Lumpkin for special effects, or to wake the congregation up, or a combination thereof, he had prearranged for Nadia Worsley to ring the tower bell at a specific time.

The good pastor gave a gentle nod in the direction of Nadi and she rose up out of the pew and gave a nod in return. The parishioners, who were still awake, squirmed in their seats. The choir behind Pastor Lumpkin scooted their robed backsides to the edge of the seats; something different was occurring! Something of interest!

Pastor Lumpkin's usual monotone drone grew louder and his voice deepened. Since he was a small man in stature, that was a monumental feat!

He tapped his fist (Pulpit pounding was not in his repertoire) on the Pulpit and spoke out, "And because of the defeat of Satan, and the joy of our salvation, I say we proclaim of the joy of Christianity and ring our church steeple bell now as a testimony of joy!"

And with those words, in the hallway behind the Altar, Nadia gave a tug on the old rope leading to the bell in the tower.

"RING! RING! RING, AND A THUD!"

A thud?

A loud thud that shook the foundations of the church. Pastor Lumpkin stopped preaching. Everyone tilted an ear and looked around at each other.

Murmurs of curiosity broke out throughout the

Sanctuary.

"What was that?"

Then another sound rattled throughout the sanctuary.

A descending, "Bang!"

The Sanctuary shook. Everyone sat in pause. Wondering.

Another descending, "Bang!"

The Sanctuary shook. Everyone sat in pause. Wondering. Rinse repeat, but the noise grew closer, and louder, and the shaking was more intense.

Then came Nadia's scream! And she burst into the Sanctuary!

"The rope broke! The bell is falling!"

Oh, no! The bell tower loomed directly above the Altar and the choir pews!

Panic ensued, and the congregation began to stream out for the exits. The young father jumped into action. He was that sort of man. He grabbed his young son and then sprinted to the Altar as the bangs grew closer and closer!

The young father hustled the choir out of the choir pews all while Pastor Lumpkin stood frozen in the Pulpit. Once the choir was safe., the young father grabbed Pastor Lumpkin, all while still holding his son, and dragged him to safety.

Once clear of the Altar, the three of them dove for cover under the first rows of pews. The final bang resulted in the ceiling above the choir rows exploding, and pieces of wood, plaster, and ceiling materials splintered in all directions. Yet, due to the holy nature of the mission of the church, divine intervention occurred. Remarkably, the bell and its enormous weight crashed through the layers of ceiling, but before crashing into the choir loft and Altar area, it stuck onto a rafter that held it firmly in its hands.

Edges of brass stuck out of the ceiling. . ..

Through the dust and mayhem, while still sprawled out on the sanctuary floor, Pastor Lumpkin looked at the young father and his son and smiled and said, "Now, that was a sermon! Knocked that old church bell right out of the tower!"

The next Sunday, for the first time in forever, a member of the Worsley family did not tug on the rope to ring the bell.

Repairs to the beloved church bell were underway.

Instead, a tape-recording of a bell ringing played.

Chuck Worsley pushed the button.

An Interview with an Evil, Mad Scientist

From: A Bowl Full of Marbles. Flashes, Sparks, and Shorts: Flash Five

The Young Reporter: (Handsome to perfection. Perfect black hair. Perfect choppers. Spray tan. Blue eyes.) "We are here today to speak with Doctor Looneytune, the world-famous evil, mad scientist. We hope to find out what he is currently working on and discover some insight into what makes evil, mad scientists do what they do. Doctor, thank you for joining us. We appreciate you taking this time to meet with us. We know how busy your life is."

Doctor Looneytune: (grey wiry hair, standing up on end as if four-thousand-one-hundred and sixty volts of electricity at a very low current charged him up. He had wild bug eyes, thick glasses. Middle age. Strange accent like he is from eastern Hudson County New Jersey, or Romania, or a mixture of both.) "You are welcome. I sure am busy these days. Working on ways to destroy the entire world is not easy work."

The Young Reporter: "Oh, my! I imagine not! And what led you to this point? Why do you want to destroy the world, Dr. Looneytune?"

Doctor Looneytune: "Well, first off, I want to destroy the world because I am an evil, mad scientist and that is what we do. I read my job description. I did not intend to do this when I found out that I was a super-genius. I wanted to do good. But the world tainted me. In school, at a young age, evil children wronged me and they teased and bullied me about my hair. I had a bad childhood.

When I was only four-years-old, that bum, Santa Claus, brought me a Purple Panda, instead of a Pink Panther. You know, all the usual stuff."

The Young Reporter: "I understand. Santa can be unreliable at times. It can be very traumatic. Especially the creeping down the chimney part."

Doctor Looneytune: "Exactly."

The Young Reporter: "How do you intend to destroy the world, Doctor Looneytune?"

Doctor Looneytune: "Oh, very easily. I will detonate my super-gluteus-maximus incineration bomb over the North Pole. Take out that unreliable bum, Santa Claus first, and then the rest of the world will fall into ashes. POOF!" (Snaps his fingers. While bulging his eyes even more than before.)

The Young Reporter: "I see. Yes, take out the cause of your pain first. And the rest of the world suffers your wrath, too. Typical evil, mad scientist behavior."

Doctor Looneytune: "Exactly."

The Young Reporter: "But won't you go POOF, too?"

Doctor Looneytune: "Oh no. I will be under my whiz-bang, super-deluxe protection dome. Unscathed."

The Young Reporter: "Good plan. Did you create that device, too?

Doctor Looneytune: "No way. Ordered that sucker on the giant internet shopping machine site. Hell-u-va good price on their special shopping day."

The Young Reporter: "I see. And that brings us to another question. What will you eat and drink if you blow up and destroy the entire world except for your laboratory?"

Doctor Looneytune: "I invented a nutrition pill, and I

stockpiled beer, potato chips, water chestnuts, and canned hams."

The Young Reporter: "Okay. All the essentials. How about funding? Where do you get your funding from for all this evil creation business and for your secret, hidden laboratory that is twenty miles under Paterson, New Jersey, and your supplies and equipment?"

Doctor Looneytune: "Oh, those ding-dongs in the government send me free funding from grants. They think that I am working on ways to save the spotted-seven-toed-blobberfish. That sucker has been extinct for ten-thousand years. The dopes did not pay attention when they read the document. Especially on page nine-thousand and twenty-two where I buried my evil intentions within the ten-thousand-page document, of which all but eleven pages are exact duplicates of the same words and paragraphs."

The Young Reporter: "Wow. Tricky, tricky. But that is what evil, mad scientists do! You sure got them good on that one!

Doctor Looneytune: "Exactly. They are all dopes, anyway. Just want to head out for cocktail hour and get free meals, spray tans, and free baseball tickets. Say, how did you know about my secret, hidden laboratory that is twenty miles under Paterson, New Jersey?

The Young Reporter: "Oh, everything is hidden underneath Paterson, New Jersey. Plus, the location is on that internet map app."

Doctor Looneytune: "Geez. I never thought of that."

The Young Reporter: "Another question. How do you not know that some double-oh-seven type of secret agent or Detective Lyle Odell won't watch this interview and foil your evil plan two seconds before detonation?"

Doctor Looneytune: "Simple. Because they are both

fictional characters, and they do not exist! Ha! Ha! Ha!" (Rubs hands together stereo-typically during evil cackle.)

The Young Reporter: "Well, technically, we are both fictional characters and do not exist either. This kooky author wrote this drivel and made us up."

Doctor Looneytune: (Looks puzzled and rubs his chin) "Well, you got me on that one, young reporter. But you know what they say, 'There is a lot of truth to fiction.'"

The Young Reporter: "You do have a point. Well, this sure has been fun and very informative, too. This concludes this interview. Right now, I will go on the internet and order one of those whiz-bang super-deluxe protection domes. I suggest the rest of the population of the world should do the same. It seems as all you did was boost the sales even more of the giant internet shopping machine, Doctor Looneytune. Thank you for your time and the shopping tip! I have tons of stock in that company."

Doctor Looneytune: "Oh no! Curses! Foiled again!" (Hand-wringing ensues.) "Did I do okay there? Were that statement and the hand-wringing perfectly stereotypical behavior of evil, mad scientists?"

The Young Reporter: "Absolutely. Perfectly stereotypical."

A Quiz on a Random Fire-Breathing Dragon Appearance

From: A Bowl Full of Marbles. Flashes, Sparks, and Shorts: Flash Five

On a hot summer night in July just 'round midnight, if a random Fire-Breathing Dragon shows up on your front lawn, at your house in New Jersey, you should:

A: Immediately run back in your house and check your homeowner's insurance policy for incineration coverage by random Fire-Breathing Dragons. Be sure to read the fine print because those insurance agents are tricky and most likely have an exemption for random Fire-Breathing Dragons that cause total incineration losses.

B: Pull out your smartphone and scroll your contacts for Beowulf's number. Give him a ring and find out his immediate availability. Remind him to bring Naegling, the dagger, Wiglaf, and tell ole Beo not to forget a shield.

C: Negotiate with the Dragon. This might be to your advantage. After all, he might be able to light that pesky gas grille on the patio that never wants to light. Or maybe the Dragon will just char-broil a batch of hamburgers and toast some marshmallows, and you and your family can enjoy a late-night snack. Or ask if the random Fire-Breathing Dragon can incinerate that pesky patch of poison ivy in the backyard that comes back every year, despite blasting it with a tanker truck load of weed killer.

D: Stop being so damn cheap and upgrade to a better quality of Scotch whiskey that does not cause hallucinatory behavior.

E: Point the Fire-breathing Dragon in the direction of your next-door neighbor's house. The neighbor who complains about your dog barking and that you play your music too loud.

D: Pull out that smartphone, pose for a selfie with the random Fire-Breathing Dragon and post it on the Zip-Zok social media site. That sucker will go viral! You might be ashes by the time it hits, but at least you go out in a blaze of glory. It is worth taking the chance of total incineration, just to get likes and to be a social media influencer.

E: Get out that smartphone again and call the Pentagon. They sure could use a random Fire-Breathing Dragon in their arsenal. Might come in very handy. . ..

F: Check for proper local laws, taxes, permits, and licenses required for random fictional characters breathing fire in residential neighborhoods. Especially, without a very difficult to obtain, Fire-Breathing Dragon permit. This is New Jersey and chances are the random Fire-Breathing Dragon has run afoul of the local laws. Nowadays there is a permit, tax, and license for everything.

G: All of the above, except for selection D. D is for ding-dongs.

A Somewhat Correct Answer

G: All of the above, except for selection D. D is for ding-dongs.

Heavenly Baseball

From: A Bowl Full of Marbles. Flashes, Sparks, and Shorts: Flash Five

Pastor Guggenheim Whorneout, had been the Senior Pastor since The Lutheran Church of the Saints, was a small, corner church on a lonely country road. In a stroke of keen foresight to the future, and led by God, the church's charter members purchased adjacent acreage next to the church property from a dairy farmer who wanted to move to Boreseville, Nebraska and start his life over. The dairy farmer's wife said he was too boring, and she ran off with the manager of the local food store.

To start a new life.

The expansion of the church was phenomenal. Who would have known that the Moondog Corporation would have built their corporate headquarters here? In Zippy, New Jersey. Now, the small town exploded and with that growth, the church expanded, too. At first, Pastor Whorneout enjoyed it. First, a larger sanctuary, then an education wing, then another school building, then a gym and fellowship hall with a full-sized kitchen. Then the Christian school. Kindergarten to grade twelve.

And along came the headaches and stress.

Pastor Whorneout had been with the church for over forty years, and now he was tired, grumpy, and had seen it all. Or he thought he had seen it all. Now, the Christian school was starting a baseball team program. Building a small ballpark right about where the dairy farmer's barn once sat on the land.

Tonight was the meeting to choose the name of the baseball team. The baseball team committee meeting. Pastor Whorneout was looking forward to this as much as he looked forward to listening to his parishioners' comment on his sermons. Another meeting consisting of church lay leaders, money families, descendants of charter members of the church, and every single one will have a different opinion. The only meeting that he could envision that was worse than this one might be was the Christmas wreath committee.

In a bountiful stroke of logic, Pastor Whorneout suggested that since the school's basketball team, the volleyball team, the checkers team, the chess team, the bowling team, the lacrosse team, the football team, and the knitting team, were all called the "Saints" that this meeting could be a waste of time, but, no, it is not that easy!

Wednesday evening. Eight o'clock. In the basement conference room. The meeting began. Pastor Whorneout scanned the room and noticed all the same arguers . . . or rather, ah, attendees.

He opened with a prayer.

In a tired voice, Pastor Whorneout prayed, "Lord, please guide us and bless us with wisdom. . .."

Mr. Pho-Fum raised his hand first. Pastor Whorneout knew he would. He always does. Mr. Pho-Fum was very zealous in the church business. He was about forty years old, owned a liquor distribution warehouse business in town, was very short, and had a bad combover. He also spoke his words with a whistle. He had a few gaps in his teeth. He and Mrs. Pho-Fum picked very original names for their children.

Fee, Fi, and Larry.

Pastor Whorneout called on him right away. Might as

well face the music right away.

Off he went, in an endless whistle of words.

"Thank you, Pastor Whorneout. I have been thinking about this for months! I made some notes. So excited! I love baseball! Here are my ideas for heavenly baseball and geography baseball!"

Most of the attendees groaned. Pastor Whorneout buckled his seat belt to prevent falling out of his chair.

With about seventy-two pages of notes spread out on the table in front of him, Mr. Pho-Fum began.

"Page one. I suggest the name of the team be The Saints. But we will also rename important parts of the game, and our team to represent our beliefs! Home plate in our new ballpark will be the collection plate. Our coaches will be pastors, and relief pitchers are angels!"

Pastor Whorneout groaned and leaned forward and rested his head on his heads, with his elbows on the table. Mr. Snickerdoodle did the same thing.

Nothing stopped, Mr. Pho-Fum. Commence whistling words.

"Page two. Hitting a homer is going to Heaven. The seats, way out in the outfields, are not the bleachers. They are Hell! Get it? Hot blazing sun. Relentless! The umpires are the Sanhedrin. Errors in the field are sins. Safe on base is a blessing. Making an out invokes automatic forgiveness. Striking out with the bases loaded or hitting into a double play requires repentance. The dugouts are the choir lofts, the young ballplayers, our student athletes are disciples and apostles. The area just beyond the outfield fences is the Promised Land and foul territory in left field is. . .."

That was all he could take. Pastor Whorneout unbuckled his seat belt; he stood up and shouted. He waved his arms in the air.

"Enough! I have had it! Over! My goodness! For the love of Saint Peter! The name of the baseball team is The Saints. All those in favor say, aye."

Every single committee member, including Mr. Pho-Fum, raised their hands and said, "Aye."

"Any nays?" Pastor Whorneout asked with bulging eyeballs, as he scanned the table, while daring any further words or discussion.

No one dared to say a word or object.

"Seeing none. It is a done deal. Fold your hands. We will now pray. Praise the Lord. Amen. The team's name is The Saints. Meeting adjourned. Good night!"

Everyone rose and began to shuffle out of the room in silence. Mrs. Wobblebutt quickly wobbled over to Mr. Pho-Fum, who had his seventy-two pages of notes under his arm and was slowly walking out of the room. Her curiosity had the best of her.

"Mr. Pho-Fum, thank you. I am a baseball lover, too. I rather enjoyed your ideas for heavenly baseball. I want to know what the names for foul territory are. But first, let me guess, the left field side is Sodom and right field side is Gomorrah."

Mr. Pho-Fum looked up and said, "Thank you, Mrs. Wobblebutt. Ah, no. Right field is Paterson and the left field is Newark. I was moving onto the geography section when Pastor Whorneout lost his mind. I was up to page three."

The next morning, Pastor Guggenheim Whorneout called the bishop of his district.

He did not hesitate one second when he heard the bishop answer the phone.

"Bishop Washboard, I want to put my retirement papers

in. Effective, hopefully, and prayerfully, before baseball season begins."

The Large Glass Window

(Previously Unpublished)

It seemed as if he had been around forever. And then a little bit more.

He knew the old cliches for change.

"Change is inevitable."

"Embrace change."

"Progress is impossible without change."

"The only thing constant is change."

He began working in corporate information technology when a bit was a bit and a byte was still a byte. They used to call him Tom; now, they called him Old Tom.

He did not mind. Instead, he laughed because, well, he was old now.

His feet hurt. His back ached, and his eyesight was poor. Staring at screens and computer monitors for over forty years will do that to you. Twelve years at one major corporation and another major corporation lured him away. Then fifteen years there. Then a director's job at a new stop; but that was high stress. Tom left that position for a new position with a lower salary, less responsibility, fewer meetings and less butt-kissing, and a whole lot less stress. But not until it cost him a marriage and more than just a few bucks of a monthly payout to the ex-wife. The price that he paid to earn a few baubles and trinkets.

And Tom always gave it his all. He was reliable,

hardworking, and dedicated. Perhaps that was his downfall. Unlike many of his co-workers and direct reports; Tom cared and always did his best.

At his new employment, Tom oversaw network, applications, and laptop and desktop support. He had a large team of fifteen technicians and support experts. All of them were good workers—smart, knowledgeable, and reliable.

The company said they cared; but Tom knew better. A worldwide corporation purchased the company, and for a few moments, Tom and his team worried about their future and their positions, but it turned out rather advantageous for them.

The company leased a beautiful new building with additional room as it grew and it grew. Tom's team found a nook within the new facility that was top-notch. A sunken floor, all painted jet-black, with a cool open ceiling concept and winding staircases, fancy workstations, a command center with monitors on the wall, tracking the network and the help desk support calls.

And the space had a large glass window that faced out into the main hallway. That might have been the best feature. Everyone would stare in and wave and make funny faces at the team. It was a window to fun and to happiness. And the big bosses could also look in and see how productive they were in their high-tech world.

It was the best of the best, and Tom and his team thrived. They enjoyed summer lunches out on the patio together, played beanbag toss in the corner of their open area, and went to happy hour at the local watering hole on Fridays after work.

It was there that Tom became Old Tom.

Some of his team left and new ones arrived, but for the

most part, the core of the team remained intact. Now Old Tom could see the finish line. He was sixty years old. He just wanted to make it to sixty-five.

The security officer out in the front lobby had seen quite a bit in his years, too. Just from a different angle than Old Tom viewed the world.

He retired from the military, and this was his second career. The security officer was a few years younger than Old Tom was, but most of his time was in the rear-view mirror and his windshield time grew less and less as he drove away the years. The security guard seemed as if he had been around forever, too.

The security officer and Old Tom got along quite well. Everyone who passed by the officer in the front lobby knew him. They stopped and chatted. He was a friendly chap; and he knew pet's names, and husband's names, and when wives were mad at their spouses, and vice versa. He handled walk-in check-ins for IT appointments and checked in all the information for remote workers whose equipment went wrong. Then, from there, Old Tom's team handled the repairs.

The pandemic came. The world went crazy! Panic and bedlam. No one knew what to do. The authorities pretended that they did! In retrospect, it would have been better if they admitted that they had no clue of what was happening.

But for Old Tom and his team and the security officer in the front lobby, it was bedlam.

Everyone will work from home!

There was equipment to check out and issue. Serial numbers to record. Paperwork to complete, cables that users required and monitors that broke.

Then, as the pandemic carried on, things smoothed out

and it became peaceful. There were appointments and equipment issued and repairs that the employees walked-in with, but it was a peaceful time.

Just the essential workers in the fancy building. The security officer in the front lobby and the mailroom folks, the housekeepers, the maintenance crew, and Old Tom's crew.

Then the bean counters crept out of the nooks to do what it is that they do.

"Wait! We don't need all these employees. . .."

Suddenly, Old Tom's team lost a few employees.

The pandemic trudged onward. Weeks became months, and then years.

Soon, it was Old Tom and just a few of his techs left.

No more lunches on the patio.

No more beanbag tosses. No more happy hours.

No more funny faces through the large glass window.

Then the pandemic ended, and the bean counters realized the error of their ways.

"Everyone! Please return to the office! But we do not need these fancy offices and areas any longer. We can all fit on one floor. Embrace the change."

Old Tom's small team, now sat in cramped desks, and what remained of the team, managed as best they could at embracing the change.

Tom thought, "Just one more year."

"Have a good weekend, Old Tom," the security officer said to his old friend, as Old Tom limped down the hallway.

"You too, Paul. See you on Monday."

The security officer stood and watched as Old Tom limped on his bad feet to the exit. On the way out, he stopped at the large glass window. He stared into what was now an empty space. A space full of cobwebs and dust. No one ever moved in after his team left.

But Old Tom remembered. The monitors on the wall. The thriving atmosphere. The fun. The people he worked with. The summer lunches on the patio, and the beanbag toss.

He gently placed his hand on the glass and felt the vibrations of the past. Even from as far away as he was, the security officer could see the tears in Old Tom's eyes.

After a few emotional moments, Old Tom turned and made his way out the exit.

Old Tom knew the old cliches for change. He also knew of and loved the large glass window that faced out into the main hallway. It was the best feature.

Everyone would stare in and wave and make funny faces at the team.

It was a window to fun and to happiness.

He just had to make it one more year.

Old Tom would. He knew that he would.

The Garden on the Hill

(Previously Unpublished)

The area seemed strange and unfamiliar to him. His home and his heart were still in New Jersey.

It would always be there.

He was in his mid-forties when he took this new job and moved to the new state. It was not entirely his decision to make; family situations forced his hand. If it were his choice, then he would have simply stayed in New Jersey.

With his beloved garden. Ah, yes. The Garden State. In his garden, he raised peppers, tomatoes, and chard, and corn. Some lettuce, radishes, and peas in the spring, some Brussels sprouts in the fall. And flowers here and there. His wife did sunflowers. She loved her sunflowers.

The garden had full sun, and it was widely productive. The man knew his gardening.

His father taught him well.

When he arrived at the new location, he plotted out the best way to drive into his new workplace. He mapped the route out on a Sunday, and he charted the best course out of a few options. His job required early morning hours, but the commute home would be during rush hour.

It was late winter when his family and he relocated. The early morning drive into work was dark and gloomy and sometimes snowy and cold. Yet, there was not as much snow as back home in New Jersey and not as cold, either.

These dark and gloomy days were the time that he combed seed house catalogs and planned his garden. Soon after came the peat pots with the seedlings under the grow lights in the late winter and the early spring.

He certainly missed his garden.

He missed many things.

On one of his first drives back home; he saw it. A garden on a hill. The gardener carved out a strategic flat spot. Even in the late winter, the man could tell that it was a good spot. Full sun.

It reminded him of his old garden back home in New Jersey. Both gardens were about the same size.

There was a small, older home adjacent to the land where the garden sat—cut into the hilly property. A red tractor stood next to a small shed. That was for turf mowing and maybe some garden tilling.

From then on; the young man kept a close eye on it.

Winter into spring.

On a warm April day, on his drive home, he spotted an older man working in the garden. Tilling over the soil. It was dry enough and must have passed the shiny boot test.

His father taught him well.

Then, a few weeks later, when the weather settled out, there were some small plants. Peppers, tomatoes; maybe some chard, or kale, or rows of corn. There were strings on racks for the cukes to climb and grow. There were some wooden stakes for the plants and a few wooden T's, a wire fence unrolled and hooked onto the perimeter stakes. Keep the deer and the rabbits out.

By early June, the garden thrived, and on his drive home, the young man finally mustered the courage to stop.

He pulled his truck into the small driveway. By chance,

the older man was working in the garden. The young man waved and introduced himself. Told the older man how he admired his garden on the hill.

And they talked about gardens. And they exchanged tips. The young man spoke of plastic soda bottle rings put around the base of the tomatoes to prevent cutworms from attacking, and of planting marigolds in and amongst the plants as companions and pest repellents. And they spoke of trimming suckers, and when to fertilize. And how to compost. Of why you water only at the roots and try not to water from above. The young man told the older man the tip of spraying Epsom salts on your peppers in late summer to turn them dark and green and to enhance that marvelous peppery aroma.

His father taught him well.

The young man told him about his garden in New Jersey and how he missed it. And the older man nodded and said that he understood. And they left as friends. Once a year for many years, the young man would stop and they talked about gardens. For hours and hours.

The young man grew old. Many things happen. He went away for a while. Then he returned. He still drove that way to work, and even if he no longer stopped to chat, he sure did admire the garden on the hill.

The older man grew even older.

Life is full of twists and turns.

Winter into spring.

Weeds now overgrew the garden. There was no red tractor. The house was empty, and a for-sale sign stood out front.

The young man was now old. He turned sixty-five that past November. On his way home one day in early April, he stopped. Slowly, he made his way over to the garden on the hill.

He remembered. He thought of the joy, the nourishment and the life that came out of that soil. The hard work that it took to make the garden thrive.

Gardens are just another gift from God.

He took his work boot and ran it over the top of the soil. The boot test. The boot mark was too shiny.

Nope, no tilling today. The soil was still too wet.

It had been a very cold and snowy winter.

Maybe next week.

The garden had full sun, so the soil would dry out quickly.

The man knew his gardening.

His father taught him well.

He wished the old man was still there and that the garden was thriving and the vegetables were full of bounty and joy.

With a few tears in his eyes, as the wind gently blew all around him, he wished that he could tell the old gardener, just one more time, how much he admired his garden on the hill.

Mr. Not Nice

(Previously Unpublished)

It was a very old city neighborhood; tucked on a forgotten side street. The houses were old; some were sad, and most had seen better days.

Many of the well-paying jobs left a long time ago, and now, everyone gets by the best that they can.

He sat on his front porch and glared and scowled at the entire world and yelled at anyone who happened to come by the front of his house, or in the street, or anywhere close by. The man kept a grouch radar always operating around his domicile. The man felt as the world had wronged him as a very young man, and he blamed the world for his feelings. He had no friends, no family, and loneliness and anger filled his soul.

People in the old neighborhood said that he did not like anything. Not a single thing in the entire world.

Some people disagreed. They said he liked beer and chocolate ice cream because that is all they ever saw him consume. He drank beer while sitting on his porch and ate chocolate ice cream. Other than those two things, he liked nothing else in the world.

Certainly, he did not like people. If he ever smiled, his face might crack.

The man was stout and squat, lumpy, grouchy, and greasy. His slicked-back hair dripped with sweat and grease in the summer months and dried up very little in the cold months of winter. His head was very large and sunk down low into his shoulders. His voice (when he did speak) was like car tires hitting gravel on the road, and his fingers were like sausages.

The neighbors spoke to him very little, and no one really wanted to speak to him anyway unless it was absolutely necessary. To the people in the neighborhood, he was known as Mr. Not Nice.

The little orange tabby kitten came wandering by one day when Mr. Not Nice was sitting on his porch scowling at the world, drinking beer, and eating chocolate ice cream. A cute, little, innocent kitten, and at first, Mr. Not Nice chased the kitten away and yelled at him.

But when the kitten kept returning, Mr. Not Nice finally decided that the kitten would be helpful in chasing the mice away from his back porch. The kitten could become a mouse policeman, and live on the back porch and do his job in exchange for food, water, and the occasional pat on the head. Very, very occasional pat.

They made a deal.

They say that eventually pets resemble their owners.

Soon, the cute little innocent orange tabby kitten grew into a large, mean, scowling orange tabby cat. With sharp teeth and large claws.

Mr. Not Nice Junior.

The cat did not drink beer, but he did eat chocolate ice cream.

The two of them sat on the porch together, scowling at the entire world.

Christopher was a friendly little guy. He was eleven years old and, despite his meager circumstances; he went through his life with his eyes wide open, and he was joyful in his approach. Christopher never knew his father; he died when he was just an infant, and his mother worked most of the time to support them.

She came home exhausted. . ..

His grandparents raised him as best they could, and they did an excellent job of doing so.

He was a little guy, slightly timid, and the schoolyard bullies often sought him out as a target.

Christopher did have a defense for those incidents; he could run really, really fast!

The little boy and his grandparents and his mother lived across the street from Mr. Not Nice.

"Hi there!" Christopher stopped at the front of the walkway in front of Mr. Not Nice's home. Mr. Not Nice and his cat sat on the porch. Glaring and scowling.

"Go away, kid!" Mr. Not Nice said with a wave as he took a sip of beer.

"Could I pet your kitty cat?" The little boy asked. "What is his name? They say your name is Mr. Not Nice. But that is not your real name. My name is Christopher."

"His name is the same as mine. Not Nice! No petting! He will hiss at you. He is just like me. We don't like anyone or anybody! Or anything!"

Christopher pointed and commented, "Well, he likes you, and you like him. You sit here together most every day. And you like beer. And you like chocolate ice cream. I've seen you eat it! I like chocolate ice cream, too."

Mr. Not Nice looked over at the cat and said, "He only likes me because he has a place to sleep and he gets ice cream once in a while. Now! Go away!"

At dinner, the little boy told his grandparents about Mr. Not Nice. They shook their heads and warned him not to talk to that mean man.

Grandpa said, "Stay away from him. That old grouch would not take kindness if you gave it to him. And kindness is free."

Grandma dished out some chocolate ice cream for them all as a treat after dinner.

"Let's save some for your mother. She will enjoy a dish when she finally gets home from work."

Christopher had an idea.

The next afternoon, the little boy stood in the same location in front of Mr. Not Nice's house. Both the cat and the man sat on the porch and scowled at the little boy. In his hands, he held two bowls of chocolate ice cream. "

"Here, sir. These are for you and your cat. I can't buy beer, so I brought chocolate ice cream."

Mr. Not Nice peered in, and Mr. Not Nice Junior sniffed in the air. Ice cream. . ..

"Why would you bring us ice cream, kid?"

"Because my grandpa said that you would not take kindness, and kindness is for free. I think that he is wrong and that you and your cat are really nice."

Mr. Not Nice thought about it for a few seconds.

Then he asked, "Kindness, huh? Your grandpa told you that? Where is your father?"

"In Heaven. He died when I was a baby."

"Your mother?"

"She works most of the time. My grandpa and grandma watch me a lot. We don't have much money. Here is your ice cream."

The little boy walked up and handed the bowl to Mr. Not Nice. Then he handed him a spoon. He set the other bowl down on the porch, and the cat jumped from its perch and dove into the ice cream.

The words did not come easily for Mr. Not Nice. But in the end, the kindness won.

"Thank you, Christopher. It is nice of you to do this. You know, my name is Christopher, too."

The little boy's face lit up.

"Cooool!"

The man once known as Mr. Not Nice smiled. His face did not crack.

He said, "My cat's name is Speedy. He runs really fast."

"I run fast, too. It helps me get away from Leon, the bully."

"Leon, huh? There is always a bully. You know, my father died when I was little, too. I understand. Maybe, well, we can be friends. Wait here. I will go get you a bowl of ice cream. Because yes, your grandpa is right. Kindness is free."

It was a very old city neighborhood; tucked on a forgotten side street. The houses were old; some were sad, and most had seen better days.

But at two houses, kindness was free.

Apartment 10D

The Space Full of Hopes and Dreams (Previously Unpublished)

There were many missteps along the way. Some were hers, but most were his.

Mistakes. We are only human.

After her marriage ended and she signed the divorce papers, she painfully, yet honestly, admitted that the marriage was a mistake.

She was always a sucker for brown eyes.

Her signature began a wave of horribleness in her life unmatched by previous waves of horribleness. This wave was the epitome of difficult times.

She packed up her past in boxes and bags and stuffed them in her car. It was her car that she was most proud of these days. She was paying for it on her own, and she intended to keep it that way. That signature gave her ex-husband most of what they had, because she did not want any of it. They would simply be very painful reminders of missteps and mistakes. No one needs those.

Yet, her car was hers.

Now, she lived in it, too.

Through it all, she kept her steady job. Thank goodness. Her debt from some of those past mistakes was now a snowball rolling down the side of a mountain. It chased her everywhere and hung like a black cloud of doom about one foot over her head. No escape.

Good and honest and loving friends helped her. She slept on some floors, some couches, some beds, and in her car. Friends let her shower and bathe and loaned her money and offered her meals.

And then there were those who posed as friends, and all they had were nefarious intentions. She was dynamic and beautiful and social. She fell in love very easily. It seemed as if love was her superpower and her Kryptonite all in one.

A few more missteps; she vowed to do better and be smart, too.

Yet, when you are forlorn and lonely, the wolves wear more than just sheep's clothing.

And then along came some temporary housing and some stability, with a roof over her head. And along came a kitten, too. A companion for the laughs and for the tears and for the good times and to hug during the difficult times.

Decision time arrived, and it was time to make a permanent move. Change is always scary.

It was a high-rise full of apartments. Full of handsome men; some with good intentions and most with nefarious intentions.

Those nefarious ones, well, they sunk into the weeds like alligators.

Waiting.

Through a large picture window, Apartment 10D had a riverside view and a city skyline, too. And it seemed as the rent was affordable. She brought along her most trusted friend for guidance and advice. Guidance and advice that she did not always listen to, or use, because she was spontaneous and carefree, and he was caring, loving, logical, and cautious.

She often threw her cares to the wind. . ..

Life with her was like riding a rollercoaster of emotions and adventures.

"What do you think?" She asked her trusted, loving, logical friend as she beamed and sparkled.

She was in love once again.

"It is my restart! My space of hopes and dreams!"

Because he immensely loved her and saw into her heart like no other friend did, even though caution fell over him like a spilled bucket of molten lava, he provided her with the same answer that he usually always did in situations such as these.

Despite his caution, he was extremely proud of her; she had crawled a long way from living in her car.

"I just want you to be happy."

She signed the lease that afternoon.

Mr. Trusted helped her move in on a boiling summer day that the temperatures were like the surface of the sun. And along came the cat.

They decorated the space full of hopes and dreams with her custom touches. Supercool lights, some old furniture, and some new furniture that Mr. Trusted bought for her. And books.

A home must have books. Or it is just not a home.

And Mr. Trusted gave her a tiny Christmas tree at holiday time.

And there were good times, and there were rowdy times, and there were peaceful times.

And there were difficult and sad times.

And of course, money was always an issue.

Mr. Trusted and his best friend tried different ways to raise money. . ..

Some worked; most did not.

And there were the handsome men.

Hordes of them. . ..

And the space full of hopes and dreams filled with booby-traps and allure. Laughter and tears.

Tears and laughter. A common combination in life.

As all spaces and lands full of hopes and dreams do.

Life is full of twists and turns. Missteps and mistakes. Hopes and dreams. Joy and sadness.

Life.

And then along came a baby. Planned or unplanned, a baby arrived on the scene. It is not like catching a fish; where you can unhook it and toss it back in the water.

She pursed her lips when she told Mr. Trusted the baby news. He did not say much.

It seemed as if he had already said it all in the past.

She was always a sucker for brown eyes.

And now, the space full of hopes and dreams closed in on her. That black cloud of debt hung lower.

It was time to combine forces. Pool money together. Babies are expensive. Time to leave the space full of hopes and dreams.

Another restart.

Her trusted friend came by and moved one of the heavier pieces of furniture, and he helped move the cat, too.

Mr. Trusted was a cat whisperer.

The cat did not enjoy car rides. He was a handful.

And she visited Apartment 10D one last time. She cleared out the last of the hopes and dreams. She might have left one dream and one hope in a hidden corner of the apartment and in her heart. For the next occupants. She felt as if she should not leave a trail of tears and what-ifs, but she had to leave some hopes and dreams.

She drew a heart on the picture window that opened to the city skyline and the river views.

A heart full of hopes and dreams.

And she knew better than to ask her trusted friend for his thoughts. She already knew what he would say.

Because he saw into her heart like no other friend did.

"I just want you to be happy."

And that is what we call hopes and dreams.

Happiness.

The Dingy Old Light Bulb

(Previously Unpublished)

The realtor called yesterday saying that he had sold the house.

Now, he just had to finish clearing it out. No easy task; his parents had lived there for over forty years. He grew up there; he recalled every memory. Both the happy ones and the sad ones.

Christmas Day. Thanksgiving Day. The famous firework displays on the 4th of July. His father's love of holidays. His mother's love in general. Dressing for the wedding. Bringing home his first date to meet his parents.

Everything.

Countless memories. As if it were a movie reel repeating in his head. His memory was very keen; that was both a curse and a blessing at the same time.

There was not much left in the basement. Just a few boxes of his father's tools. And the workbench.

The dingy old bulb hung over the workbench by a thin black rubber cord. It had a small shade on it, a thumb switch on the side. It always swung side-to-side when you had to operate the switch. A person needed to place their hand on the shade to steady it to flip the thumb switch.

The bulb and the shade had a coating of dust and memories. He stood there staring at the dingy old light bulb and the workbench.

Here come those memories.

He stood still there for a few minutes.

The New York Yankees banner still hung above the workbench.

In his mind's eye, he could see his father there. Right next to him, working on the workbench, and he was just a little boy, standing right next to him with tears in his eyes. His father worked feverishly to repair his son's toy soldier that had fallen apart. Parts and pieces were all over. It seemed hopeless; but in his father's skilled hands of a machinist, underneath that dingy old light bulb, there was hope.

"Wounded in combat," his father said.

In a few minutes, the soldier was back in action. The soldier's head bent at a weird angle and it no longer swiveled, and his right arm tilted at an angle, but he was now a grizzled veteran of war. As his father was, too.

Then there was the rising smoke of a soldering iron, as together, father and son assembled the shortwave radio from a kit that changed the boy's life.

When the radio jumped to life and they tuned in the signals, they hugged in love and accomplishment.

And there were water pumps and exhaust system parts, and a steering box that they banged on and sprayed penetrating oil on the frozen bolts to fix the 1964 Rambler.

And the struggles and combat with old water pipes and motors, and swimming pool filters and a washing machine pump. And assembling his sister's fashion model doll's dream house. A million parts and pieces.

Then the endless bicycle flat tires.

The taping of friction tape on the handles of baseball bats. Varnishing those same bats to preserve them.

And taping the blade of his hockey goalie stick. It deadened the puck; helped with the rebounds.

Let's not forget gluing together the precious broken pieces of porcelain on a family heirloom.

Epoxy was his father's key weapon in the repair arsenal.

He reached over and turned the dingy old light bulb on as he supported the swinging fixture with his other hand.

It did not throw much light. It never did.

That is what the flashlights were for.

He stood there and allowed his eyes to study the workbench. All the nooks and carvings on the surface. All the memories. All those repairs and projects. They were both a curse and a blessing.

He could hear his father's voice. He recalled the endless lessons. How to use tools. How to fix things; experiences and lessons that no school or instructor could ever teach him. Now, he knew all of those lessons, too. He passed on to others the lessons that he could, but he could never replace the lessons learned over that old workbench.

Under the dingy old light bulb.

He wiped away the tears from his eyes. He recalled all of it all too well. The dingy old bulb hung over the workbench by a thin black rubber cord. It had a small shade on it, a thumb switch on the side. It always swung side-to-side when you had to operate the switch. A person needed to place their hand on the shade to steady it to flip the thumb switch.

The bulb and the shade had a coating of dust and memories. He stood there staring at the dingy old light bulb and the workbench. With a painful movement, he reached out and steadied the light fixture. He flipped off the thumb switch.

Very carefully.

The last thing that he wanted to do was to disturb the dust and memories.

Thinking Like a Fish

(Previously Unpublished)

Henry retired four years ago. He worked for over fifty years at a plastic factory. Earned a decent wage; banked a few dollars; lived within his means. Took good care of his wife and two children. As best as that decent wage could do.

Now, when the yard work was all complete on their postage stamp city lot, and the chores all complete, and Henry was getting on his wife's nerves, Henry grabbed his fishing pole and headed for the local pond.

The pond was the Oldham Pond. Named after a long-forgotten section of the old city. The state stocked it with trout in the spring; by June they were gone, but the bass, the sunfish, the catfish and calico bass and the yellow perch remained. It was a fun place, where a trophy fish might be out of the question, but the peacefulness was always there.

Henry had a decent set of tackle. It was over thirty years old, but the reel was smooth as silk.

He caught quite a few fish at the Oldham Pond. He had been fishing here since he was a young boy.

Henry knew the hot spots and the cold spots, and he knew the secret spots.

The little girl looked as if she lost her puppy dog. She sat on an upturned plastic bucket that was sitting on the walkway around the pond. She held her head in her hands, and active and dried tears intermittently graced her cheeks.

She had brown hair in pigtails, and she wore a sweatshirt and a pair of blue dungarees.

On her lap sat a kiddie fishing pole with the logo of a popular cartoon character emblazoned on the pole and on the sides of the closed-face fishing reel.

Henry came along with his tackle box in his left hand; he held his fishing pole in his right hand, and around his waist was a belt with a creel with some bait sitting inside.

Henry stopped and studied the little girl. He recognized her as being a nearby neighbor's little girl. The family lived a few doors up from his house. He did not know her name, but she always waved and smiled at Henry. Henry was the kind of guy that everyone waved and smiled at.

"I know you, but I don't know your name. You live by me. Why are you so sad?" Henry asked. "You should be happy. It is summer vacation. It is a beautiful day, and it is a perfect time to go fishing."

The little girl looked up and said, "I know you, too. My mother and father always say that you are a nice man. You are always cutting your grass in the summer and shoveling snow in the winter."

"Well. Thank you. I guess that is very true that I am always working in the yard. There is a lot of work to do around the home."

She said, "I am crying because my brother and his friends are mean. They made fun of my fishing pole and said that I have to fish over here where there are no fish. I have not caught anything with my junky fishing pole. And I don't know what to do."

Henry looked around the pond and saw a group of boys fishing not too far away, casting under a few overhanging branches of trees overlooking the pond's water. He surmised that the little girl was about ten years old and her brother and his friends might be thirteen or fourteen.

The brother was close enough to keep an eye on his sister. . ..

"And where are you fishing? I just see you sitting on a plastic bucket," Henry said. "There are no fish there."

The little girl pointed at the pond in front of them and said, "I was fishing there. I can't get the line in the water, so I quit. My pole is junky."

"Oh, I see." Henry walked over and set his pole and tackle box down next to where she sat, and he stuck his hand out and said, "Hi there. I am Henry. The man who is always working in the yard. Thank you for always waving and smiling at me."

"You are welcome. You are nice to smile and wave to. My name is Vicky. Victoria."

She shook his hand like she meant it.

"Beautiful name. Would you like to fish with me? That pole looks like a fine pole. My first fishing pole when I was your age was a broomstick with a string tied on the end and a bent sewing needle for a hook. I had no money for an actual fishing pole."

Vicky's little eyes lit up.

She jumped off the bucket and said, "Yes! I would like to go fishing with you. Wow! And you caught fish with it?"

"Sure did. You see . . . it is not about the fishing pole. Please. Let me teach you a secret. To catch a fish, you have to think like a fish."

Little Vicky grabbed her pole, and Henry grabbed his gear, and they made their way to the side of the pond.

"Huh? What do you mean, Mr. Henry? I am a little girl. Not a fish."

"Okay, got it. Is it a bright sunny day out, and is the sun strong and hot? Does it make you hot and a little sweaty, too?"

"It is hot. Yes."

Henry pointed at the pond and said, "Well, even though the fish live in the water, the sun can make the water warm, and the fish can't see what they want to eat in the bright sunlight. They move to where it is cooler and a little shady."

The old fisherman looked up and scanned the water and pointed to a small section of the pond where the water tumbled off onto a runway of a man-made cement waterfall.

Henry explained and pointed.

"Right over there. The running water is cool. And if you sit there in the cool water, all the water in the pond runs to you. And anything good to eat that is floating in the water comes to you, too."

Henry turned to Vicky and asked, "Do you have any bait?"

"Yup. A yucky worm. My brother put it on the hook for me."

Henry leaned and studied the worm as the little girl held her pole up in the air for Henry to see the dried-up old worm on the hook.

"Oh my. I see. Would you eat that? I mean if you were a fish? Because to catch a fish, you have to think like a fish!"

Vicky shook her head and said, "I don't eat worms. But if I were a fishy, I would not eat that yucky thing."

Henry smiled. Vicky was cute, and she was smart, too.

"Exactly. You are very smart. Here. Let me have your hook."

Henry reached into his bait box and pulled out a small wiggly red worm. He cleaned the old worm off Vicky's fishing hook and hooked the red worm on the hook, and began his lesson.

"Now, stand here, Vicky. You don't need much line. Just push the button on your reel and let it go when you wave the pole in the air. Let the line go right in that pool of water there before the water runs really fast."

Vicky nodded and, with a bit of surprising skill, she did exactly what Henry said. Not perfect, but the worm and line were in the water. The bright red and white plastic bobber on her fishing line landed with a little splash.

Henry stood next to Vicky and pointed and said, "Watch that bobber. If it sinks under the water, you pull back on that pole and start to reel the line in."

The bobber sat for a lifetime. For about three minutes. It floated around in the gentle currents like a happy little red and white bobber.

Ten-year-old children are impatient. . ..

"Ugh, Mr. Henry. No fish!"

"Watch the bobber, Vicky. Good things come to those who wait."

Henry might have said a little prayer.

Suddenly, the little red and white bobber dove under the surface of the water! The little cartoon fishing pole bent at the tip like a shepherd's hook!

"Pull back, Vicky! Reel it in!" Henry shouted.

The excitement hit both of them, and the struggle began. Henry watched and helped as Vicky reeled the fish in.

It was a fine yellow perch. A beauty! About ten inches of golden and yellow delight.

Vicky beamed as Henry helped her bring the fish to the bank of the pond. He lifted the perch in the air and proudly displayed it to the little girl!

"Wow! I caught a fish! I caught a fish!" Vicky shouted as her brother and his friends all dashed over from where they fished close by them.

"Now, Vicky. Let me take this perch off the hook. As I taught you, you have to think like a fish. What should we do next?

Henry very carefully worked the hook out of the fish's mouth. Her brother and all the boys stared in and celebrated with the little girl.

"Mr. Henry. If I were that fish, I would be scared and want to go home." Vicky turned and pointed at the water and said, "There."

"Exactly," Henry carefully leaned over the edge of the water and gently released the perch into the water. They all watched as the fish darted into the cool, deep water.

He added, "The fun is in catching them. . .."

Suddenly, everyone fishing in the entire pond were casting their lines into the spot where Vicky caught her fish. It was bedlam.

Henry leaned over to Vicky and her brother and the boys and he asked, "If you were a fish, would you stay here now?"

In unison, all of them shook their heads no.

Henry smiled and said with a wave, "C'mon. I know another secret spot. I know all the secret spots here. Been fishing here since I was your ages."

They all smiled and jumped for joy with their poles in their hands. Henry was the kind of guy that you wanted to smile at.

Vicky ran after Henry and asked, "Mr. Henry. Are you gonna fish, too?"

"Oh. I don't know. Maybe Vicky. When you get old like I am and have fished all your life, you tend to catch a lot of fish. Sometimes it is more fun to watch and teach young children about fishing than it is when you actually fish. Joy and kindness and teaching young folks—well, that is worth more than all the gold in the world."

He caught quite a few fish at the Oldham Pond. He had been fishing it since he was a young boy.

Henry knew the hot spots and the cold spots, and he knew the secret spots.

He was all too willing to give up those secrets.

And he also knew two other secrets. One: to catch a fish, you have to think like a fish.

Two: something about joy and kindness, and teaching, and gold. . ..

The Banana Split Finish

(Previously Unpublished)

It was the moment of truth. Years and years of practice. Countless hours on countless ice rinks around the world. Grueling practices since they were youngsters. Injuries, ice packs, sprained knees and ankles, cuts, and bruises. Broken fingers and toes. Endless doctor's visits for repairs. Hours and hours, and days and weeks, and years, of weightlifting and cardio-conditioning. Practice, practice, and more practice. And now it all came down to this. For the gold medal! To walk into history. Forever!

"And here they are," Blabber McGee, the television commentator, spoke into the microphone. "The team of Ivan Carrottopski and his partner, Lily Looseyasagooseylegs, from the remote country of Upper Zoolakia, for the doubles ice-skating championship of the world! Can they overtake the team of Loopy Bamboosil and Sniffy Snozzoly from Iceloffskia? Can they execute a perfect performance and win the gold? What do you think, Q-T?"

The old ice-skating color commentator, Q-T Expert, growled into the microphone.

"I don't think so, Blabber. It will take a remarkable performance with an amazing finish to win it all. When I won my gold back in the 1911 Games, with my partner, Mary Goodytwoskates. . .."

"Okay, yes, Q-T. Yeah, yeah, yeah. Enough of that story.

We have heard that boring story before. In fact, a few thousand times before. Here they go! It is a great start for Ivan and Lily! Great selection of the music. The theme from the movie, Pillows on our Butts! Strategic. Okay, very smooth, a quick double flippity-doo-dah. Very well done! Followed by a twirl-de-la-whirl-a-roo-ski. And lookie at that! A hot doggie with some spicy mustard on top move. That is gonna cause some heartburn later tonight! Perfect so far! They are both picking up major speed around the corner. They must need some speed for the next move. Oh, no! Look there on the ice, Q-T! Dead ahead of them! What is that?"

"Well, Blabber, it looks as if Old Leo the Zamboni driver must have had his lunch while he resurfaced the ice, and he accidentally dropped his old banana peel on the ice! Could be a tricky situation."

"Here they go! I don't think they see the lost banana peel! Up in the air! They both hit it with their skates! Up! Up! And lookie there! A quad-ripple-de-la, flippie, double flewwie with a banana split finish! Holy guacamole! Never before ever attempted, nonetheless executed successfully in competition! I think they have won it! Yes! Perfect tens!"

"Well, Blabber, ya just never know in sports. They turned a potential slip-up into gold! Remarkable! I never would have thought they would have attempted the treacherous banana split finish and pulled it off."

"Q-T. I must ask. Do you think Old Leo, the Zamboni driver, was in on it? I mean, it seems awfully suspicious for him to lose that banana peel right there in that section of the ice."

"Well, Blabber, ya just never know in sports. . .."

The Perfect Job

(Previously Unpublished)

"Well, Mr. Cantankerous. It seems as if you have had quite a few jobs over the last few years," the interviewer commented while glancing at Mr. Harvey Cantankerous's job application and the attached resume.

"Please call me, Harvey. Yes, I am still trying to find my niche in the employment world."

The interviewer nodded and quickly counted the jobs listed on his resume.

Fourteen jobs in the last six months.

"Okay, well, Harvey . . . it is then. Why do you want to be an amusement park ride operator?"

Harvey Cantankerous immediately answered.

"It seems like a fun atmosphere to work in."

The interviewer nodded and agreed.

"Yes, it is! Please let me ask you a scenario question. You are the ride operator on the Loop-De-Loop from Hell amusement ride, and a rider, a young man, is screaming his lungs out and is frightened to death. He is screaming for you to stop the ride and let him off. What do you do?"

Harvey Cantankerous immediately answered.

"That is easy. I push the speed button or lever and increase the speed and leave him on the ride for even longer by pushing the extend button on the ride timer.

Teach him a lesson not to be a cupcake in life!"

The interviewer immediately answered.

"Thank you for stopping in and for your interest in the job, Mr. Cantankerous . . . ah, Harvey. I don't think this position is a proper fit for you at this time. . .."

The interviewer glanced at Mr. Harvey Cantankerous's resume and spoke, "You do have to deal with quite a few elderly people here at the pharmacy. They might not see so well and might need some assistance with reading information labels and have many questions. How do you enjoy customer service and dealing with elderly or confused customers?"

Harvey Cantankerous immediately answered.

"I can't stand dealing with dopey people. I would tell the elderly person the truth. I'd say, look ya old bag, it ain't my problem that you are blind as a bat. Go buy a pair of reading glasses and read the label yourself. Or better yet, go to an eye doctor and get your eyeballs checked."

The interviewer immediately answered.

"Thank you for stopping in and for your interest in the job, Mr. Cantankerous . . . ah, Harvey. I don't think this position is a proper fit for you at this time. . .."

The interviewer glanced at Mr. Harvey Cantankerous's resume and asked, "Why did you leave your last job, Harvey? This position you had as a funeral home attendant at the Very Saddykins Funeral Home."

Harvey Cantankerous immediately answered.

"They fired me. They said I wasn't sad enough. All because I told a crying little boo-boo cupcake at his uncle's funeral to quit crying like a big baby. Hs uncle was one-hundred-and-two years old. What did he expect? The old guy finally keeled over and croaked. Nothing to cry about."

The interviewer immediately answered.

"Thank you for stopping in and for your interest in the job here at The Sympathy Center, Mr. Cantankerous . . . ah, Harvey. I don't think this position is a proper fit for you at this time. . .."

The interviewer, Mr. Waldorf Curmudgeon, glared at Mr. Harvey Cantankerous's resume and asked, "Do you like people and helping them?"

Harvey Cantankerous immediately answered.

"I generally can't stand people, and the last thing that I want to do is to help them."

Mr. Curmudgeon smiled and nodded.

Mr. Curmudgeon asked, "Other than the extraordinary pay, the endless holidays, the short workday, and the glorious benefits, why do you want to work here?

Harvey Cantankerous immediately answered.

"Other than what you mentioned, I can't think of a single reason."

Mr. Curmudgeon smiled and nodded.

He said, "I see here that you list under your job skills that you excel at being miserable." Then, he asked, "On a miserable mood scale, where the number ten is miserable and the number one is super-unbelievably miserable, where would you place your usual daily mood?"

Harvey Cantankerous immediately answered.

"I am a solid one. I can guarantee that if you put me up one-on-one against your currently most miserable employee, I would, hands down, whoop them in a misery contest."

Mr. Curmudgeon smiled and nodded.

He said, "A scenario question. A customer walks up to your counter and says, 'I really need to get this done today. Even though my grandmother is in the hospital, and I took a day off from work to get here, and my house flooded from a broken pipe, and I just waited in line for three hours to get here to the front counter . . . I need some help with the forms. I am not sure that I have all the correct information with me. Can you please help me?'" Mr. Curmudgeon swallowed and then asked, "What would you say to that customer?"

Harvey Cantankerous immediately answered.

"I would tell that idiot customer that none of that is my problem. If you don't have the proper information or the forms filled out properly, then you can go home and get the information and figure it all out on your own. We aren't a help desk here. I would then wave the dopey customer aside and would yell very loudly, NEXT!"

Mr. Curmudgeon smiled and nodded. He then stood up from his chair, reached over the desk, and very enthusiastically shook Mr. Harvey Cantankerous's hand.

Mr. Curmudgeon shouted out his response!

"Fantastic! This is the perfect job for you! You are hired! In fact, if you keep the proper demeanor and show up at work at least half of the required days, I can see you being a manager here in six months! Welcome to the front desk clerk position at the State Department of Motor Vehicles!"

The Last Hurrah

(Previously Unpublished)

The twenty years had gone by in a blur. He hardly recalled most of them. It was just a joyous journey through the words.

Father Time; undefeated.

Imaginations are powerful tools for a writer.

When the joyous journey of the words slows or ends, the writer begins to see things other than words.

"Are you finished?" She asked as she watched him type the last few keystrokes on the keyboard, and throw his head back, then rest his head on his chest.

His breaths came in great heaves; then his chest settled. It had been such a long road. Now, he arrived at the end.

He closed his eyes and then opened them and looked at her standing beside him.

She had never looked so beautiful.

He looked at her and smiled and said, "I think I have finished. It is the last hurrah for me. I don't think that I have anything left to say. I guess that I turned off the lights now. Yes. Done. Have you been here the entire time? I mean . . . throughout all these words? Through all these books? While I typed all these words? This entire time?"

She smiled and moved close to him and threw her arms around his neck as he clasped her hands and he lowered his head.

He gently kissed her hands.

"I have. You just never noticed me until now."

"That so?"

"Yes."

"I wonder why?"

"Because there were so many words. So many things that you had to say. I waited for you to finish. It was worth the wait. You are worth the wait. Our love is worth the wait."

"Thank you. I love you."

"I love you, too. And if you decide to turn the lights back on, then I will be here, too. Now, and until the end of time. To the last word."

He smiled.

It was all that he had left to do. To smile. There were no more words left to write or to say.

At least, none for now.

She smiled back.

A Short in the Circuit

The Row of Honor

(Previously published in When Words Fall Short)

"My dear, Pastor Paul, your schedule this week is one horrific mess after another."

It was early in the morning, on a Monday, during the first week of May and I had just made a rather captivating cup of tea, settled into my office chair to sip it and try to enjoy it. I looked over my teacup at my longtime, faithful, and marvelous assistant, Ms. Martha Wiggins, and gently shook my head. Instead of taking the long-awaited sip of tea, I placed it down upon the coaster on my desk, folded my arms across my chest and waited.

As I mentioned, Martha was my longtime, faithful, and marvelous assistant. She was famous for her forthright ways, and her rather honest and "unfiltered" manner of speaking, as well as her reputation for being rather tough. We worked together for many years at Reunion Lutheran Church, and when I received the promotion to the Office of Bishop of the Northeast Lutheran District, I asked Martha to join me here in the same role. We were a team. Honestly, I would not know what to do without her.

Martha knew that I disliked the title of Bishop Henson; therefore, she still utilized the Pastor Paul title when she addressed me by name. Martha knew everything about me. I do mean everything.

Martha looked at me, shrugged her shoulders and said, "We have not been together for as long as we have for me to sugar-coat my statements for you, my dear Pastor Paul. I ran the church office at Reunion Lutheran Church like an efficient machine for all of those years, and now that we are here together in the bishop's office, I am doing the same thing for you."

"Thank you, Martha. I genuinely appreciate your honesty and frankness. Even on a very early Monday morning, after I had a glorious weekend with my wife and children, and have not had more than a few glorious moments to bask in the afterglow of family-related bliss. The dose of honesty, even before I have had even a sip of this glorious tea sitting and steaming away in front of me, is truly heartwarming."

"You are most welcome. Someone must remain grounded around here, and not expect Heaven to intervene on our behalf every ten minutes or thereabouts, to save your confused ass. By the way, this scene reminds me that Mrs. Henson called late on Friday and asked me to monitor your tea intake. Her latest research indicated that experts consider the amount of tea that you suck down these days to be well more than the recommended guidelines for a man of your age and size. Mrs. Henson believes it is a direct cause of your chronic insomnia, too."

I had just placed my fingers on the handle of the teacup and was going to take a sip when Martha relayed the latest statistics from my research-obsessed wife.

Martha leaned back in the guest chair and shook her head while once again, shrugging her shoulders. I sighed, took my fingers off the teacup, and gently pushed it aside.

"Hey. Do not blame me. I am only the piano player. I did not write the music, Pastor Paul. I only relay this because I love you."

I nodded, pushed the teacup even farther away and mumbled, "I love you too, Martha."

"How many cups of tea did you have before you left the house? I bet you had two already."

"Yes, two. Actually, no . . . three. This one would be four."

"See. Mrs. Henson is correct. She usually is. She loves you, too."

"How much sleep did you get last evening?"

"About three hours or so."

"Ah, huh, yup. Her research is right on."

I frowned at Martha. She laughed, waved her hands in the air as if to dismiss my frown, and she picked up some papers that she placed on my desk.

"Now, that we have your well-being out of the way . . . let's get you on the right track to bedlam."

She picked up her eyeglasses off the desk, put them on, and stared at the paper. My assumption was that this paper contained the "horrific mess" of a schedule for the upcoming week of which Martha had previously warned me.

"First off, I will skip the rest of the week. It is so busy that I doubt you will have time to suck down tea, pee, or even eat. Ah well, maybe you might have time to pee. Instead, let's just get through today. Now, I know that Pastor Lysling Junior wanted you to visit his church on Memorial Day, but that day has been booked ahead of time for you for close to two years. I told him that I would get you out to his church as close to that day as was possible. However, today was the best that I could do." Martha looked up at me as if to gauge my reaction and when I did not actually have any reaction, she continued, "You do know, Pastor George Lysling Junior and Our Redeemer Lutheran Church of Golden Lake? Don't you, Pastor Paul?"

I sat in my chair. Frozen. Stupid look on my face. As I said, Martha knew me rather well.

"Pastor Paul, you have no idea of whom or of what I speak of. Do you? Do not bullshit me. I know you too well. That cute face of yours when you try to fudge stuff, your eyes, they are windows to your soul."

"Can I have a sip of the tea, Martha?"

"No! Our Redeemer of Golden Lake in Golden Lake, New Jersey. Warren County. Way out near the Pennsy line. Small church. Only one hundred or so members on the roles, maybe thirty, show up at the service. Pastor Lysling Junior took over for his father."

I slowly shook my head, gently pointed with one finger at my teacup, and gazed lovingly at Martha.

"Oh, go ahead! Your good looks and puppy dog eyes are hard to resist. Do not tell Mrs. Henson and blame me when you never sleep. I never want to hear you utter a single word about how you cannot sleep. Not a syllable. If you do so, then I will have a protest day, unplug my computer, not sort mail, or answer the phone for the entire day. I also will head to the corner pub and have a liquid lunch on your tab."

"You have been sent straight from Heaven to me, dear Martha. You really have."

"I know, and sometimes, I wish I could fly back up there to get away for a little while. It would be wonderful to sit and relax on a puffy-white cloud, sip a triple Tom Collins cocktail, and watch while my kids, my husband, and you, spin in the wind because Martha and Mommy are not around to save their little, confused, and perplexed asses. Yet, despite my dream, with your heavenly connections and superhuman abilities, I know that would be futile. I know that because you would end up there with me, asking me to find a phone number that I have already given to you ten times before or to help you find your portable communion kit, ten seconds before you have to leave for a hospital sick call. Now, listen carefully while you suck down your insomnia juice. I booked you for a noontime arrival out at Our Redeemer. The church is in a very rural area, off the beaten path, far from our offices here in downtown Newark. I have printed a color-coded map for you, and in a little bag on my desk is a healthy snack for you to munch on while you ride out there. No stopping for tea along the way. In that old piece of junk jeep of yours, if you leave now, you might just make it in time."

I smiled because I loved Martha Wiggins.

For the first week or so of May, it was a bit on the cold side. The sun hid behind some clouds here and there, and when the sun was not shining brightly, it was, indeed, quite cool outside. I did not mind; I loved the cold, snow and ice and I always felt a tinge of sadness when the spring decided to leave and give way to the generally disgusting heat and humidity of summer. I tooled along in my old bucket of bolts of a jeep. This old wreck and I had traveled far and wide, and it was a part of my soul. Money was not the issue. I could easily afford ten new jeeps for a poor kid from the old neighborhood. Success had not arrived quickly, but I had found it. As did my lifelong best friend, Harry M. Redmond Junior. We often sat and marveled at how far we had journeyed from such humble roots. It had not been easy. It required an awful large amount of pain and sacrifice for us to reach this point. As much as I should consider a new vehicle, I always balk before making the move. Someday, not right now. A new jeep would not have the character, the stamina, and the history of this one. Someday, when the wheels roll off, the poor undercarriage falls out on a road somewhere and I am left sitting in the driver's seat holding the steering wheel in my hands, in and amongst the rubble, then I will cry like a baby-boo-boo and finally concede that it is time for a new one.

Until then, we are a team.

Martha was, as usual, right on in her description of this being a long ride from our offices. First, after resisting a stop or two for another cup of tea, I made my way along Interstate Route 80 and then, while following Martha's map; I exited and rolled along a rural road or two, or three. Anyone who judges New Jersey by what they see along the New Jersey Turnpike will understandably develop some false misconceptions about what New Jersey is really like. Off the beaten path, just a few hours, or thereabouts, (if you drive as I do, then it might be more) you will find one of the most beautiful areas in the entire world. On this final leg of the journey, I had to study the map a bit more carefully, therefore; I stopped along the side of the road, put my flashers on and endured New Jersey drivers beeping their horns and shaking their fists at me for stopping them for two microseconds on their travels. Even after seeing me dressed in a black suit and my pastor's collar, the drivers did not stop the glares of disdain and hurling of obscenities. Perhaps my appearance with long blonde hair, a full beard and my overall "hippie" appearance made them think that I was an imposter.

Who knows?

This is rural New Jersey, and the locals out here in the country had no time for a city slicker from Paterson and Newark, who could not find his way along their country roads. There were cows to milk, and trout to catch. I imagined that I could hear them scream as they passed me, "Ya bum, ya drive like an old lady. Get the heck outta the way! Lutheran bishop or not!"

The map promised me that the winding country road I was currently driving on was the last road on my journey. The way-finding signs perched along the roadside which advertised on a backdrop of the logo of the Lutheran Church, the whereabouts of "Our Redeemer Lutheran Church, 3 miles ahead," also confirmed that Martha had once again been invaluable.

While I wandered along, shamefully burning excessive oil into the atmosphere with my worn-out pistons, I felt a bit of shame at the fact that I had been in the bishop position for over two years now and until this day, had never visited this church. I faintly recalled the pastoral calling process and installation service for Pastor Lysling Junior after his father retired, and if I recall correctly, Pastor Lysling Senior passed away shortly after that. I did not attend the installation services; I approved the paperwork, signed off on his appointment, but due to another conflict, Pastor Paul skipped out on attending his installation. As Martha and my loyal wife, Binky, painfully reminded me quite often, there was only one of me. Too much work, not enough time, yet, I still felt ashamed.

There were a few other churches on my circuit that I still never visited as of yet. I spoke to these pastors on the telephone, exchanged correspondence, but never met them in person. Shameful fact. Pastor Paul John Henson, you need to do a much better job.

Along a slight curve in the road, just beyond a long portion of bumpy asphalt, I spotted the church and, while signaling my turn, I turned the jeep into the driveway of Our Redeemer Lutheran Church. A glance at my watch told me that I was ten minutes early. Since there was only one other vehicle in the entire parking lot, and it had a specially issued New Jersey "Clergy" license plates, I made the simple assumption that Pastor Lysling Junior was around here somewhere. I parked, grabbed my Bible, and picked my black suit jacket off the passenger seat along with a folder of paperwork, which Martha told me that I would need to give to Pastor Lysling Junior. In one quick motion, I jumped out of the jeep and made my way to the facilities.

For a country church in the middle of a very rural setting, the church was quite impressive. I glanced up at a proud, tall, flagpole that appeared as if it had just received a fresh coat of white paint. The pole proudly displayed a crisp American flag, which was flapping in the breeze at the top of the mast, with the Lutheran flag mounted just below it, and then below that flag, flew the POW/MIA flag.

While I walked along, I slipped my jacket over my pastor-collared shirt and scanned the building and grounds. I had to admit that the church was just a bit larger than I had expected it to be. Admittedly, it was a lot more appealing than I had envisioned it, too. It was tall, stately, impeccably maintained in the appearance of both facilities and landscape. The church building joined a small wing that was obviously a newer addition of, perhaps, a meeting hall, some classrooms for use by the Sunday school and some offices. What I perceived to be the sanctuary had stark white clapboards for siding with stacked fieldstone foundations. This church was old; very old. I guessed it to be from the mid or early 1800s, but diligence and many generations of congregations full of love and care had preserved it as a testimony to the glory of God. There was an assortment of large oak doors, with gorgeous stained-glass windows depicting Bible scenes, reflecting the sunlight of this Monday in early May. Most of all, what caught my eye was an impressive bell tower that guided the path to Heaven and beyond, while it towered above me. I stood in the parking lot, next to the beginning of a sidewalk; leading to what a small sign on a post shown was the walkway to "The Church Office."

"Bishop Henson! Say, over here! Sorry that I was not here to greet you more formally. You are early and I was busy in the cemetery. Tending to some needs out there."

Two steps up the sidewalk and I paused to try to locate the person shouting my name. Amongst a rustle of leaves in a gentle breeze, from what seemed to be a forest of tall oaks and maple trees, which towered over me, the voice seemed to be lost.

I finally spotted a very short, thin, somewhat frail looking, middle-aged man with a shiny baldhead, wearing a black suit and pastor's collar, not unlike my own, hustling his way towards me.

I stopped, smiled and when he came close enough to hear me above the rustle of the wind in the trees, I said, "Pastor George Lysling Junior, I am Pastor Paul John Henson. Please, just call me Pastor Paul. Never became comfortable with the Bishop Henson title."

Pastor Lysling Junior smiled. He stopped, and it was then that I noticed he was wearing work gloves, or in fact, more accurately, he wore a pair of gardening gloves. He removed the gloves, placed them in his left hand and with his right hand reached out to shake my hand.

"Oh yes, another apology is in order. I feel so discombobulated. In my mind, I made such glorious plans to meet you with some hot tea or coffee and be ready for your honorable visit, but the graveyard and my gardening duties captured me. Your assistant, Martha Wiggins, instructed me, or more accurately lectured me, to call you, Pastor Paul. I apologize because I blew it. Please do not tell Martha . . . she seems . . . a bit tough. Slipped my mind. Please, it is my great pleasure to meet you. I am Pastor George. I enjoy that simple title, apparently just as you prefer, too."

We shook hands, for such a smallish man, and as I mentioned, somewhat frail looking, his handshake was very powerful. His hands were rough, calloused, and a bit gnarled. His small hand eclipsed inside of my giant hand and when I sensed his grip was strong, I carefully, yet powerfully shook his hand.

From his jaunt, he was still a bit out of breath, yet his face was glowing in his enthusiasm, his smile was infectious and I found myself smiling with him.

Pastor George spoke, "Wow! Other pastors in the circuit, and people who have met you before me, told me to be prepared because you are large, tall, strong, and imposing, but I must say that even with that prelude for an introduction that I underestimated your size. My goodness, you are a large man! All the hair and beard and such they told me about, too. The descriptions were correct."

"Please, thank you, but no apologies are necessary. I will not reveal anything to Martha. Yes, she is tough, but amazing. I would be lost without her. To tell the truth, in fact, I owe you many apologies. Most of all, for taking such a long amount of time to arrive here, to meet you and to tour your amazing facilities. Most of all, I have been wayward in visiting, in order to thank you and thank God for your hard work out here. I am very sorry, no excuses are available which are valid, but this office has been a bit of a challenge to handle. Much more so than I thought it would be."

Pastor George pointed up the sidewalk, in the direction of the steps, and he placed his hand on my back as we walked, in order to guide me along. While we walked, he took me a bit by surprise with his comments, not that I did not just admit to my inadequate performance, but maybe, a slight sense of ego at my lofty office, would not expect a direct report of mine to agree with me in the entirety of the statement.

"Apologies accepted. I wondered what it might take in order for me to meet our leader and my boss. I heard from my father that your predecessor, Bishop Von Houten, spent quite an awful lot of time on the golf course rather than in the office, so, initially, it was difficult for me to imagine what occupies your time so much. Also, I heard that Bishop Von Houten was quite a character. Yet, my father always spoke very highly of him. Dad told me that despite his gruff exterior, and what people perceived to be a lack of commitment, Bishop Von Houten was an impeccable man of God. I never met the man. As you might recall, I was working in Wisconsin for most of my career."

"Your dear father was correct. Bishop Von Houten is a great man, he is a dear friend of mine, and I owe him more than I can ever repay for all that he did for me."

I now placed his accent. Wisconsin. My mind reeled as I tried hard to recall his biography. Sadly, I was not recalling too much.

Pastor George smiled and continued to state his position with my waywardness, "When you only sent letters and cards when Pastor George Lysling Senior passed away, and I received the calling here to replace my father, then I thought the best course of action would be to take matters into my own hands. Therefore, I decided to invite you out here to visit by telephoning you directly. Even when I did so, I only had the pleasure of speaking with Martha. She is quite efficient and a bulldog when it comes to guarding you."

I nodded and did not immediately comment. I guessed that I might have been reeling a bit at the honest and forthright agreement by Pastor George of my performance. Deserving, no doubt, still the words stung a bit.

"Pastor Paul, well, Martha is very good at what she

does."

"Martha is the best. Yes, in my case, my feeble efforts at some types of successes are in a large part, due to several great women who back me up and keep me charging forward. In my case, Martha, my lovely wife, my daughter, and my best friend's wife. They are my support team in a journey of faith. They all are much smarter than I am or will ever be."

We climbed a short staircase together, Pastor George laughed, opened the door for me and between laughs he told me, "Yes! Good move, Pastor Paul! You are smarter than you give yourself credit for because you know enough to elevate the women in your life above you."

We stepped inside. The office was perfectly suited for the church. It was clean, neat, and brightly lit. Pastor George's desk was neat as a pin, not a paper or pen was out of place on it. Bookcases covered the walls of the office and countless books were all jam-packed into the shelves of the bookcases. It was hard for me to imagine or try to guess how many books there might be stacked in them. It was very impressive, and for a voracious reader and hapless writer such as I was, this was an incredible amount of reading material. The sight of all of this material made my eyes widen, and my heart race at the thoughts of such a vast reading opportunity.

"Please, sit there in the guest chair. Would you like a cup of tea or coffee? It would just take me a minute to prepare on this little hot plate here," Pastor George spoke, while he opened a drawer behind his desk in a small upright cabinet.

A drawer that with my height, I could see contained all types of tools, some haphazard assortment of parts and repair supplies, and other items. He tossed his gardening gloves in the drawer and closed it. It was then that in my thick head, I realized that Pastor George was everything here at Our Redeemer Lutheran Church of Golden Lake. It now made sense why his hands were strong, rough, calloused, and a bit gnarled. This was a different world than my background was, or most of our churches were. He was the pastor, leader, gardener, administrator, preacher, maintenance and janitorial, all wrapped up in one person. No highly efficient, Martha Wiggins sat outside his office to keep him on track, organized, and take care of everything for him.

He was a one-man band.

My eyes caught a can of white paint with a paintbrush sitting upon the lid, tucked neatly in a corner next to the same cabinet, which housed his tools.

It appears as if he paints flagpoles too.

"No, thank you, Pastor George. I will skip the tea and coffee. I am, as Martha and my wife had double-teamed me today and informed me thereof, well over my daily limit of caffeine already. I am an insomniac and those two are trying hard to have me cut back on my tea intake."

"Oh, I see. My wife used to harp on me for my coffee consumption habit, too. Now, I wish she were here to do so. You might or might not recall that I am a widower."

He studied my eyes for a reaction.

I felt as if honesty was the best way to go here, and before I could even say that I did not know that and extend my condolences, Pastor George jumped in and let me off the hook.

"No trouble. You might have missed that rather easily. She passed long before I took this position. A long, wretched battle with breast cancer. It is in my biography, but it was when we were living and working in Wisconsin." He finished speaking and sat in his chair behind his desk. He took a pen from a cup and fiddled with it a bit.

"Pastor George, I have to say how very sorry I am to hear of that. It must be very difficult."

My eyes studied his nervous habits, and I was just about to change the conversation when he spoke again.

"It is difficult. I miss her every day. She died in May. In a week and a few days, it will be the anniversary of her passing. While we are men of God, we are just that, Pastor Paul. Men. When you lose a love, a woman who was pure grace and goodness, it makes you doubt your faith, the plan, and your life's work . . . it stops your world from turning. Some days, I want to tear this collar off and pack it away in a little box. Then, I come in here and it brings me back to the true Gospel. It grounds me here. A few minutes ago, I was a little difficult on you, but the truth is that I do know what occupies your time."

I leaned back in my chair. I had to admit; this man was quite the conversationalist. He had the gift of speech and he now had me intrigued. The way he shifted gears on me caught me leaning.

"You are, without a doubt, an amazing man. As my office reveals to my visitors and now tells you, I read all the time."

He waved at the rows of books and smiled as he continued, "I tucked volumes of your work in there, too. I love your books, your dissertations, and your sermons are the best that I have ever read. I cannot even tell you how I have dissected your sermons and tried to duplicate your thoughts from my own pulpit. My sermons proved to be fruitless efforts. You are the best. We, of course, never met in person before today, but I feel as if I know you so well. The word prolific does not capture the vastness of your work and the word inspirational does not describe it.

Driven, endless, wide, and a broad thinker and a man of superior insight into God's world and our roles within the same, does capture some of it. In addition, I know that you are a tireless worker. You had not made it out here as yet, but that is no fault of yours. You are only one man, and there is no question that you took the bishop's office to a new level."

I sat there, stunned. A few short minutes ago, I received a well-deserved roundabout criticism or two.

My usual long-winded tendencies caught me as I started to speak, but once again, managed to be slow on the draw, "Why, my goodness, thank you but. . .."

"Your biography is unbelievable. A professional hockey player, to pastor, to bishop. Rising out of the streets of Paterson, tough and unforgiving. Very impressive. All of us pastors—we talk. We are sinners and we gossip. You know, the strange people in our congregations, the holier-than-thou lay leader leading a life of lust and deceit, while pinching his secretary's backside on the sideline of his life, and, of course, we talk about the boss. I heard the snickers about you from my fellow clergy. Longhaired, hippie, pastor. A terrible New Jersey accent tinged with highlights of Welsh and English from his heritage. Cawwwfee, holy wadder, dawgs and his dawwter, all framed by an occasional eh, and a few English cuss words. A rock and roll guy. Hockey player. Now, you are a bishop! A man of God! What kind of nonsense is this? They snicker until those who have met you, or read your works, pipe in there and tell them about the real Pastor Paul John Henson."

"Pastor George, you humble me with your praise and words. I am positive that I do not deserve them, but nonetheless, I do my best. Thank you for the kindness and understanding. I do work hard, feel ashamed that I do not have the time to do all that this office requires, or cover all that it needs to cover. All we can ever do is the best that we can do. We all fall short, every single day."

I waved my hands in the air as a signal to end this portion of the discussion because I wanted this visit to be about this church and this humble pastor's mission. Most of all, I wanted this visit to be about what I could do to support Pastor George and his congregation.

"Enough of me. Please, now, tell me about this wonderful church. How are you doing? It is old. Very old. Please, tell me all there is to know."

"Built in 1845. The cornerstone tells the history. New Jersey protects this building now as a historical site. Built by German farmers and some Scandinavians. Proud, honest, we have a hundred and four church members. They support the church and while the attendance for our worship services is not in any manner very overwhelming, the power of the Gospel is strong here. This is rural New Jersey, Pastor Paul. These families and people would never understand *your* New Jersey. Not the crime, the grit of city life. Yet, my hope is that after today, you understand *their* New Jersey. We are more than just farms, rural life, and trout streams. This New Jersey is all about some other things too. We know about serving God and country and about pride, appreciation, and respect. That is why my father felt so at home here. That is why I had to come to this place too. It was easier after my wife passed, for me to leave Wisconsin behind me in the rear-view mirror, but please understand and know that there are much more here than just an old church and historic building. Please. Leave your folder with the office mumbo-jumbo here on my desk. I know what is in there. Martha briefed me. Come along with me. Let me show you around."

I followed Pastor George for close to two hours as he showed me every inch of the church and the adjoining building. He explained what his role here was and why he felt it was so special. He was correct because it was more than special. It was a beautiful inspiration in its finest and purest form. The sanctuary was marvelous. Awe-inspiring. I could feel the presence of his congregations of the present and of the past, and while we toured around, I could feel his passion for this church. I missed one of his duties. As well as gardening and the other tasks, Pastor George even played the church organ during services. His "choir" consisted of four members, and one of them was Pastor George. When we completed the tour, I felt humbled as well as impassioned by this incredible man's dedication and deep faith.

With a smile of satisfaction upon his face, he leaned on the wall of the narthex, crossed his arms, and asked me, "You have asked such in-depth and honest questions, but as yet, you have not asked why it was that we wanted you to visit Our Redeemer Lutheran Church of Golden Lake on Memorial Day. That was my initial request to Martha, but she rather sadly reported that you were unavailable for that date."

I nodded, honestly, that question was there in the back of my mind, but first, I wanted to ask Pastor George if there actually was a Golden Lake, but instead, my thoughts wandered and I commented, "I was coming around to that. I think that it might have something to do with the fresh coat of paint on the flagpole out there in front of the church. Is that so? I have a feeling that with the hinge mounts at the base of the flagpole, and the can of paint and brush that I spotted in your office, you tilted the pole over a few days ago, and freshened it up a bit, eh? No doubt, as a prelude to an upcoming event."

"You are even keener than your reputation tells of you. I find it very interesting how you study everything before you speak or comment. Your eyes follow everything, and the writer and storyteller in you gathers in all the environments that surround you and absorb all the words that people speak. No doubt that you will use them later on in a story somewhere down the line. You are very perceptive. Please, follow me out to the graveyard. I want to show you another reason why this place is so special. Another aspect of Our Redeemer Lutheran Church of Golden Lake that most people are not aware of. What I meant when I mentioned the honor here."

Pastor George took a few steps, unlatched some dead throw locks on the front door, and pushed the heavy oak door open. The sun had now chased around the corner of the church, making its way to the cradle of the sky where it would sleep until morning.

Pastor George stopped in his stride. He glanced up at some more clouds slowly gathering in the sky. Clouds, which now covered a great deal of the sunlight.

He looked at me and asked me, "Do you require a heavier coat? Did you leave an overcoat in your jeep? You and I only have our suit jackets on and I feel as if the day is growing colder."

With a shake of my head, I told him, "No. I am comfortable in the cold. I seldom, if ever, wear an overcoat."

He nodded and waved me on.

With a few quick steps from his short legs, his polished black shoes with dried licks of telltale mud on the edges of the soles from his gardening stint, hit hard upon the step-stone path leading to a graveyard behind the church.

He called out while he led me on, "We have much in common. That makes sense . . . a hockey player. Have to say that you are a handsome man. I heard that all the ladies swoon at the sight of you. I do not have that influence on the ladies. As a lonely widower, sometimes I wish that I did! Ha! No, no, no, it is actually quite the opposite, but you are indeed quite a representative for the Office of the Bishop. Yet, in the sunlight, I can see the scars of a hockey goalie who wore a mask, combined with some pain of life on your face, too. I enjoy the cold too. I am still a Wisconsin man. Wisconsin is hockey country. I was a very good ice skater at one time too. I would love to swap some hockey yarns with you some day. I must say—the colder the better, Pastor Paul. The colder, the better."

"Pastor George, let's do someday chat a bit about hockey. Wisconsin is beer country too. Perhaps we can sip a few and swap hockey stories. Maybe a skate someday. We would both enjoy that, eh?"

He did not comment, but waved again for me to follow.

I followed him and the path was too narrow for us to walk side-by-side, so instead, I fell behind him and we made our way to what was a small graveyard behind the church buildings. It was quite a bit smaller than I expected, with a black iron fence lining the entire perimeter. A black iron fence without a spot of rust upon it and, as the flagpole was, the fence proudly wore a fresh coat of paint.

I knew the identity of the painter.

The grounds between the gravestones were a display of impeccable grooming. Even though it was still early in May and the weather remained cold, the grass in this part of New Jersey was slowly growing and while it was not in full-growth, it required some maintenance.

Once more, I knew the gardener too.

Rows of gravestones lined up in straight and perfect rows. I glanced at the names. German, Swedish, some English, some Welsh, and a few Danes. Typically, Lutheran. We wandered along until Pastor George led me to a row of gravestones. This row of markers was the longest in the entire graveyard, and Pastor George marked each gravesite with American flags.

"Here we go, Pastor Paul. It is what we call around here, The Row of Honor. Our veterans. Unofficial, someday we might research it, but for no other reason . . . other than just to know. Unofficial, but for the size of our burial grounds and our very small congregation, we feel as if we have more combat veterans and other veterans buried here per square yard, than any other church graveyard in The United States of America. Unofficially. I have nothing to base that upon other than hearsay. However, what does it matter? You can look and see for yourself. Over fifty graves in The Row of Honor."

We walked along very slowly. I felt a shiver go up and down my back, and it was not from the breeze or from the chill of the waning day. It was from the honor and from the sound of the small American flags flapping in the afternoon breeze.

I shook my head at the incredible display of generations of heroism in such a small location.

Vietnam, World War Two, World War One, Korea, The Gulf War, The Spanish-American War. Navy, Marine Corps, Army, Coast Guard, Merchant Marine, Army Air Force and Air Force.

"Incredibly, we have combat veterans and other veterans of every war, every era, except for, The American Revolutionary War and the Civil War, buried here. We missed those. Not by too much, but we did."

"These were all members here?"

"Most of them, Pastor Paul, but some were relatives of members. Not all were combat casualties, but most of them were."

I mumbled, "Remarkable," while I stopped and kneeled on the hallowed ground. There, I silently read the words from a stone marking the grave of a Coast Guardsman, killed in action, in the Pacific during World War Two. Next to that grave was the grave of a soldier killed in trench warfare in France during World War One. Men and women. It was a touching display of honor and patriotism. Right here, in a tiny graveyard of a small Lutheran Church in the middle of rural New Jersey.

The sun escaped the clouds, and it shone down upon us brightly. It seemed as if the golden rays filtered a glow of celebration upon the graves of these heroes and heroines. I stood up and squinted in the sudden broadcast of sunlight, as I tried to look to the end of The Row of Honor. Reaching into my jacket pocket, I took out my sunglasses and placed them over my eyes.

We continued to walk, and it was then that I noticed a grave at the end of the row, which had fresh mounds of flowers gathered upon it. Even with my sunglasses on, Pastor George must have caught my eyes searching for it. He motioned for me to walk ahead of him because he sensed that I was going to inquire about the new grave. We reached the end of The Row of Honor and he pointed down at about fifteen or so grave markers in a line within the row.

"I am no expert and it is simply my opinion here, but I have to say that this is one of the most profound displays of patriotism anywhere, or any place. This line of markers . . . they are all the grave markers of the graves of one family. The Hendrick family. A very large family. Some of them signed the church charter here. These graves are an incredible testimony of courage, honor, and love of this country. See there for yourself. Read all of them there, Pastor Paul. All of them, some going all the way back to The Spanish-American War. The Hendrick families were amongst the original settlers in Warren County. Farmers. Mostly. However, they all knew honor and commitment. Read 'em. Starting there with Wilhelm Hendrick. He died in The Spanish-American War. Then one of his sons, killed in action in World War One. Next is an uncle lost in the Great War. It keeps going. Generations of 'em. They just kept, and in fact, keep serving."

I walked along, studying the markers. Two brothers lost in World War Two, and what appeared to be uncles and cousins all lost in World War Two. Some, Navy. Some, Army. A Marine. Then another Hendrick lost in Korea and three more in the Vietnam War. The Tet Offensive. I knew of some war stories of that one and a few more war tales too. Our old neighborhood had more than just a touch of honor and we had our heroes here and there, too.

We reached the fresh grave, and I looked at Pastor George for his explanation. I could not read the marker because the mounds of flowers covered it over. He reached down and picked up a few flowers that the breeze had blown off the pile, and he tossed them back on top of the pile. When he looked back at me, he had tears in his eyes.

"This is where I was when you arrived. I had some last-minute attention that I needed to give to this grave. This morning, I admit that I also prayed here for a very long time."

Pastor George pointed at the grave and said, "Another Hendrick. Airman Kyle Hendrick. He died at the end of last week in an accident on an air base in Texas. A terrible accident. He was only twenty-two. He was an acolyte for my dad here. Dad, well . . . he baptized him and confirmed Kyle too. The honor made him enlist. The tradition. The commitment. His honor to God and to our country. We cannot measure this or understand it . . . nor honor this all enough. A year or so ago, he had met a lovely young woman from over the river in Pennsylvania. A few months ago, Kyle proposed to her, and she accepted. I counseled them about their pending marriage. Kyle wanted to settle into life in the Air Force before they married. His loss has greatly affected me. Pastor Paul, it has made me doubt our faith . . . it is so disturbing to my soul."

His testimony instantly disturbed my soul, too. My heart sunk and I searched for some reason, some words to explain the meaning to all of this. I could not find anything but did the best that I could.

"I am very sorry. Very sorry. You are correct in saying that we cannot measure his honor. We need to pray together in honor of his life and his service. For his willingness to be a part of The Row of Honor."

His face reflected profound pain and, in an effort to absorb some of that pain, I gently placed my hand on his shoulder to support him.

"Please, Pastor George, please, you must try hard not to have any doubts, and take solace in the fact that by your commitment to being an advocate for God's ultimate plan, you will forever honor Kyle's glory. No doubt, God required an airman for his angel's corps and Kyle is now serving in the ultimate ranks of service. The great majority of people only take from this great country, and never realize the commitment of so few, to protect the freedoms and the glory. This young man—he understood. He was one of the few. His commitment will remain forever. He was willing to stand in defense and in honor of these freedoms. We can never repay sacrifices of this magnitude. We can only honor it."

"Thank you, Pastor Paul. I will now take solace in your glorious words."

I motioned to him that we would pray.

Pastor George kneeled, and I kneeled beside him. I reached for his hand, and he clasped mine as we fell to our knees in front of the fresh grave. I removed my sunglasses and together, hand-in-hand, we prayed for this young man's life, for his fiancé, for his family, and most of all, for his courage and commitment to God and our country.

"Father in Heaven. We cannot even begin to pretend to understand why you took a proud young man such as Kyle from this world so early. We have faith that you needed him in your Kingdom, but we still struggle to understand as to why he had to leave his family, his love, and his friends still here on Earth, grieving his loss. Jesus wept, too. Perhaps you required his courage in Heaven for a purpose, for part of your plan. Regardless, we thank you for his life, for his honor, and for his sacrifice. We know that while we do not understand, we have faith to accept it and that due to Kyle's honor and sacrifice, we will move on in our journey of faith. We will never forget, and we will remain steadfast in our service to your kingdom. In Jesus' name, we pray. Amen."

We stood on our feet, and in silence, faced the grave.

Pastor George spoke first.

"Thank you for such a bold prayer, Pastor Paul. Honestly, I expected that level of boldness and forthrightness from your heart and your soul. Honesty is something that you wear on your collar, and courage pervades you. You have the courage to admit that you do not understand God's plan. Do you agree with it?"

"No, how can I? When you see a grave such as this young hero's grave . . . I do not agree. Yet, I trust and obey."

"You are painfully honest and I respect that fact, Pastor Paul. I really do. Thank you for your words and for sharing your deepest thoughts."

"You are welcome, Pastor George. Even Jesus, when faced with the cross, asked in an honest manner if there might be any other way. Then he, as we try hard to do, trusted and had faith. I must say, thank you for such an amazing day of enlightenment. You reminded me of something that I needed reminding of. Sacrifice in the purest form is one of a human being's greatest attributes. So, few are willing to do it, especially with so little of a personal reward attached to it."

If I could, I would kick my own ass, for my earlier thoughts of thinking that growing up in the old neighborhood had elements of sacrifice and pain, yet, when compared to the pain and sacrifice on display here, our commitments were feeble and miniscule. I could also kick myself for not coming out here earlier, and I vowed in the future to do a better job.

Pastor George looked at his watch, and then to the sun, which was thinking of setting now and said, "Yes, well, I am sorry it is so late now. I know that you have a long ride back."

I looked over at the sunset and admired the golden rays illuminating the top of a row of oaks towering above the cemetery. A bright and golden sunlight bathed the leaders of the trees while the trunks were now in some elements of darkness. I slipped my sunglasses back on; there was still enough sunlight to bother my light-sensitive eyes.

It was now time, so I decided to ask the question that I knew that I had to ask, "Where in the cemetery is your mother and father's grave? I would like to pay my respects. Please, can you take me there?"

Pastor George's head whirled around and he stopped in his tracks with a look of shock on his face.

Once he steadied himself, he asked me, "How did you know that my parents are buried here?"

"Because of your parent's combined honor, your father's honor, and of the honor of this congregation, and . . . because of yours."

He shook his head, and again, I saw the tears form in his eyes.

"There is no doubt whatsoever that the hand of God is upon you, Bishop Henson. Please, let me honor you and call you that title just once. I will take you there. I picked the location. It is in this far corner near the end of the fence line, just one row over from The Row of Honor. I selected it because the sun is usually always shining in this location. Even in the winter when the angle changes."

I nodded and accepted him, calling me by my formal title.

Just this once.

I prayed at Mrs. and Reverend George Lysling Senior's grave, paid my respects, and agreed with his son that it was a fabulous location.

While we walked back to the church buildings, I asked Pastor George, "What time does the service begin on Memorial Day?"

With a wide and glowing smile, a smile of relief, a smile of joy, he quickly answered, "We start at sunrise. You will need to leave Newark early."

"I live in Great Falls. The office is in Newark. Our home is fairly close to the interstate. I will be here."

"Thank you, Pastor Paul. That will be very special and I doubt that I will be able to explain how much it will mean to me, to my father, to us . . . and . . . to them. Say, I was wondering if you could help me with a little piece of advice on something?"

I nodded and gently said, "You give me far too much

credit. I will be here. I feel it is a miniscule contribution in light of the incredible sacrifice on display here, but I will be here. As far as helping you, of course, I will try to help you. However, I am not sure of what I could help you with, but I will give it a whirl. It might be the other way around, but. . .."

"You might have noticed that The Row of Honor is almost to the end of the limits of the graveyard. Someday, realistically, it might reach the fence line. Technically, the limits of the graveyard are the fence line. The Church owns many acres beyond that fence line. Many. When we reach the fence line, do you think we would then need to begin another row? It would be a shame to break up the row."

Instantly, my old Paterson, New Jersey street sense, kicked in. God could polish me up, make me a professional goaltender in hockey, make me a pastor, a leader of numerous folks, then decide to turn me into a bishop, but in reality, I never left those old, gritty city streets.

I smiled, put my arm around him, and whispered, "Well now, I think we will keep that between just us. What certain people do not know or realize will never hurt them or come into play now, eh? After all, we can move that fence line just a little and I am sure that no one would ever notice, eh? For what they have done for us, we should move Heaven and Earth and a few fences, too."

Pastor George's face broke into a glorious smile. He enthusiastically grabbed my hand and shook it hard.

"I can tell that you are from Paterson! That works for me, Pastor Paul!" He then turned and stared over in the direction of the cemetery and mumbled, "For some reason, they just keep on comin' here. Not too sure why, but they do."

I, too, looked over at the sacred burial ground, then looked at him and answered, "I think that I know why. It is because of the honor."

I rode back home and wished that I was riding into the west, but home and the office lay due east of Golden Lake. I would have enjoyed the last remnants of today's sunset.

In my rear-view mirror, I could see the last rays of sunlight with touches of gold, some red and a little yellow, licking the horizon behind me. Honor, commitment, sacrifice. Thank goodness for those who were brave enough to be willing to give all of what they had, so that we could enjoy all it is that we enjoy. Thank goodness for wonderful men such as Pastor George and his father, who recognized that sacrifice and were willing to do everything to preserve their honor forever.

Prayers are not enough.

Words are not enough.

We always fall short.

All we can do is to remember and honor.

I thought about how I never asked if there actually was a Golden Lake, but I made a mental note to ask Pastor George about it on Memorial Day.

I turned the jeep onto the interstate, shifted gears, and slowly climbed up to highway speed. What a glorious day this turned out to be! No matter what the "horrific mess" of a schedule that awaits me for the rest of the week, at least I will have this day and the emotional memories and inspiration it brought to my soul. As the old jeep rolled along, the aggressive treads in the jeep's tires made a slapping noise on the highway, and for some odd reason, I thought how wonderful it would be to have a hot cup of tea right now. I know that after today and the wave of emotions that were sweeping over me, another cup of tea would not make much of a difference.

There was no way that I would sleep very much tonight,

anyhow. Tonight, I had some work to do. First off, I had to practice my "puppy dog" eyes in an effort to ease into the conversation with Martha, of having her rework my schedule for Memorial Day. Then, and more importantly, in my mind, I had to plan exactly how we were going to move that fence.

After all, just as Pastor George reminded me of today, I am from Paterson, New Jersey, ya know. . ..

THE END

ABOUT THE AUTHOR

If you ask Paul John Hausleben, he will tell you that he is not an author, he is just a storyteller. His mission is to continue to write and tell stories to warm your heart, make you laugh, make you think, and sometimes make you cry, just a little. Most of all, he deals in memories, and helps you to remember the good times of your own life, and the special people who touched you along the way.

Mr. Hausleben's writings cover a wide variety of genres; with his many novels, his flash fiction pieces, and short story collections, touching the genres of fantasy, military stories, humor, nostalgia, holiday and Christmas stories, crime-drama, and mystery, and even some touches of romance!

Paul was born and raised in Paterson, and then nearby Haledon, New Jersey, and began writing at an early age. He revisited a writing career later in his life, and he now is the author of several novels, compilations, short stories, music reviews, and audio and video works. Most of his work touches upon nostalgic remembrances of simpler times, and tells the stories of heartfelt, humorous, and special human relationships.

Mr. Hausleben is the Flagship Author, and the driving creative force of God Bless the Keg Publishing LLC. Paul is a skilled photographer, and God Bless the Keg Publishing LLC features much of his photographic work. He is the host of God Bless the Keg Publishing LLC's podcast. Other than writing and photography, among many careers both paid and unpaid, he is a former semi-professional hockey goaltender, a music fan and music reviewer, and an avid ice hockey, football, soccer, and overall sports fan. Paul is an avid supporter of the Nottingham Forest Football Club. He is a former military radio operator, and a current and very active and avid amateur radio operator. He holds an extra class amateur radio license with the call letters WA2ASQ and he is a Morse code and digital mode operator. Paul enjoys on-the-air radio contests and chasing long distance (DX) stations from all over the world.

Mr. Paul John Hausleben now resides in Somewhere, U.S.A., but his heart always remains along Belmont Avenue in good old Paterson, and Haledon, New Jersey.

Other Work by Mr. Paul John Hausleben

The Time Bomb in The Cupboard and Other Adventures of Harry and Paul

The Night Always Comes, Another story from the Adventures of Harry and Paul

Reunion, A sequel to the Night Always Comes and Another story from the Adventures of Harry and Paul

The Miracle Tree, Another story from the Adventures of Harry and Paul

The Chronicles of Henson

Heaven's Gain

The Final Adventure of Harry and Paul

Geyer Street Gardens

Beneath the Mask of a Hockey Goaltender

Another story from the Adventures of Harry and Paul

Where the River Bends and Curls

Tales of the Quiet Stranger in the Black Hat

Crows on a High Wire

A New Jersey Christmas Tale

Christmas Cocktails

Flashes, Spark, and Shorts: Flash One and Flash Two and Three, Four, and Five

Experiences: A Series of Essays on My Life

O'Malley

The Many Cases of Detective Lyle Odell

And many other too!

You may write to the author at ctte27@gmail.com

Published by God Bless the Keg Publishing LLC

Henrico, Virginia, U.S.A.

You may write to the publisher at
Godblessthekegpublishing@gmail.com

"Life's simple pleasures are so often the best ones!"

Follow Paul John Hausleben on Facebook and enjoy samples of his photography, receive updates on new releases, and enjoy his general meanderings. Follow Paul John Hausleben and God Bless the Keg Publishing on our YouTube and our podcast channel, too!

Book reviews are important to authors and publishers! Please consider leaving a book review for this publication on your favorite book website, blog, or publication. Thank you.

www.ingramcontent.com/pod-product-compliance
Lightning Source LLC
LaVergne TN
LVHW040222110826
845146LV00004B/1257

* 9 7 9 8 9 8 9 4 4 9 0 5 7 *